"I'm a fun date. You'd have a good time. There's got to be somewhere in town you've always wanted to go but haven't gotten around to. Tell me what it is and I'll take you tonight."

Darcy was about to shut him down, but as she stood there looking at that half-playful, too tempting smile all she could think was how long it had been since she'd really had fun. Of all the things she'd told herself she'd get to some time but had never managed to do.

Now her time was up. She was leaving tomorrow.

Jeff was offering her a chance to— God, was she seriously considering this?

She never said yes. Never gave in and did the fun thing for fun's sake. Maybe tonight, after living the straight and narrow for so very long, just this once she could afford to break the rules without worrying about tomorrow.

"I'll think about it."

Dear Reader

It's no secret that I'm all about the Happily Ever After. I like my true loves and for evers big, beautiful and wrapped up with a gorgeous bow—preferably the kind that comes with a sparkly diamond ring or maybe even a baby on the way.

Now, normally I make my heroes and heroines work for those fairytale accompaniments. But for some reason when I started playing with the idea of best friends Connor Reed (WAKING UP MARRIED) and Jeff Norton (WAKING UP PREGNANT) I couldn't resist mixing things up by giving these guys the traditional happy endings at the beginning of their stories!

Of course a ring alone or even a baby on the way doesn't guarantee for ever... But with heroes as charismatic, determined and resourceful as these two you can bet they'll be pulling out all the stops to earn that hard-won Happily Ever After we dedicated romantics thrive on.

I hope you'll enjoy reading Jeff and Darcy's story as much as I enjoyed writing it.

All my best

Mira

PS If you haven't read WAKING UP MARRIED, no worries. While the stories are loosely tied together by one fateful evening in Vegas, they can most definitely stand alone.

WAKING UP PREGNANT

BY
MIRA LYN KELLY

MILLS & BOON

Published in Great Britain 2014
by Mills & Boon, an imprint of Harlequin (UK) Limited,
Eton House, 18-24 Paradise Road, Richmond, Surrey, TW9 1SR

© 2014 Mira Lyn Sperl

ISBN: 978 0 263 24186 0

Mira Lyn Kelly grew up in the Chicago area and earned her degree in Fine Arts from Loyola University. She met the love of her life while studying abroad in Rome, Italy, only to discover he'd been living right around the corner from her for the previous two years. Having spent her twenties working and playing in the Windy City, she's now settled with her husband in rural Minnesota, where their four beautiful children provide an excess of action, adventure and entertainment.

With writing as her passion, and inspiration striking at the most unpredictable times, Mira can always be found with a notebook at the ready. (More than once the neighbours have caught her, covered in grass clippings, scribbling away atop the compost container!)

When she isn't reading, writing or running to keep up with the kids, she loves watching movies, blabbing with the girls and cooking with her husband and friends. Check out her website—www.miralynkelly.com— for the latest dish!

This and other titles by Mira Lyn Kelly
are available in eBook format
from www.millsandboon.co.uk

To Eleanor, Joyce, Jessica, Elizabeth and,
kicking off the fourth generation…Jacqueline

CHAPTER ONE

WITHIN THE FAST closing walls of his downtown L.A. executive office—a modern, stylized space reflective of his personal tastes, professional achievements and global priorities—Jeff Norton watched the limitless sky of his future crack and crumble as the woman in front of him doubled over, one arm clutching his trash can, while the other shot straight. Her hand alternating between a traffic cop's stop signal and a single finger indicating it was going to be a minute before she got to him.

"Not a problem, Darcy," he managed in a voice barely recognizable even to himself. "Really. Take all the time you need."

The sounds of distress emanating from the depths of his violated wastebasket ceased and the Vegas cocktail waitress he'd found too tempting to resist three months ago pinned him with a watery stare before rolling her *you-did-this-to-me* eyes in disgust.

Which was almost enough to pull a laugh from him, except, yeah, that look said it all. This was the end of days.

Probably.

Because while it wasn't any great mystery as to why this woman was seeking him out now, months after those fateful few hours they'd spent together that ended with him staring down in abject horror at what could best be described as an epic latex fail, whether the hormone-wreaking miracle behind this reunion was, in fact, his, or whether his portfolio simply made him the most obvious solution to a problem which might be laid at the feet of any number of other candidates, was still yet to be seen.

Though even as he thought it, something inside him rebelled at the idea.

Three months.

If she'd been here after one... Hell, if she'd still been there that first night when he came back from the bathroom...

He swallowed. Sucked a deep breath, only to realize what a monumental mistake he'd made when the smell permeating his office—his sanctuary, his power position, his godforsaken happy-place-no-more—had his stomach contracting in some kind of sympathetic reflex.

Darcy looked over the plastic liner at him and, seeming to catch the wayward direction of his stomach, tightened her hold in a move very obviously saying, *Get your own can, buddy.*

Nice.

His molars ground together. This was the mother of his child.

Maybe.

Crossing to his desk, he dialed his assistant's extension. "Charlie, I need a bottle of mouthwash, a toothbrush and paste and a dozen trash liners. And if you can get it all in here in the next five minutes I'll cut you a check for a thousand dollars today."

Darcy pinched her eyes shut a moment and when she looked back at him, it was with reluctant gratitude. "Thank you."

"Suppose it's the least I can do...." Considering what he'd *maybe, probably* done already.

He watched the rise and fall of her shoulders as she struggled for her composure.

"I'm sorry—"

He waved her off, but her eyes narrowed so he let her go on. "About springing...this on you. It must...be a shock."

More so now than it would have been two months ago.

"We can talk about it after you've had a minute to yourself. There's a private bathroom back this way. Charlie's freakishly efficient—"

As if underscoring his point, a knock sounded as the office door swung open for the fastest man in the West, who'd somehow managed to collect a tray of the requested items along with an unopened sleeve of saltine crackers in a matter of seconds. Considering Charlie normally coordinated international business meetings, spoke seven languages and had an MBA from the top school in the U.S., the toiletry run wasn't perhaps the best use of his time. But for Jeff, the guy had just come through in what ranked up there with a life-and-death emergency.

"Charlie Litsky, this is Darcy—" And there it was, the glaring reminder he didn't even know her last name. Right. Moving on. "Darcy, Charlie," he said, leading them back to the private bathroom in the far corner of the office.

"Why don't I take this?" he said, relieving a sallow-cheeked Darcy of the trash can at the door. "Before you leave today, I'll give you Charlie's contact information. If you need to get ahold of me, or anything else, he'll be able to help you."

But then Charlie produced a card of his own, already inked in with a private mobile number. The man was worth his weight in gold. Proven even more so, when they excused themselves to leave Darcy at the bathroom and Charlie eyed the trash Jeff was holding at arm's length.

"Can I take that for you?"

Jeff blew out a humorless laugh. More than anything he wanted to say yes. But whatever the actual protocol for vomit in the office was, Jeff couldn't stick this with someone else.

Holding out a hand for the liners instead, he shook his head. "This is my mess. Think I'd better be the one to clean it up."

Darcy Penn glared into the mirror in front of her, scrubbing the foul taste off her teeth and tongue with a vigor fueled by humiliation and outrage. One that wasn't going to get her anything but gums that wouldn't grow back if she didn't ease up a little.

The nerve.

He'd referred to her as "his mess." And offered *his assistant's* number in case she needed to get ahold of *him.*

What an ass.

And to think she'd been afraid of seeing him again. Worried she'd find herself susceptible to the same judgment-obliterating spell she'd fallen under that last night in Vegas when she'd found this guy so unbelievably compelling, she'd essentially broken every rule she had, just for a few hours with him. Anxious the man whose easy charm and demanding kisses infiltrated her dreams with nightmarish frequency would be as irresistible as she remembered him. And once again, he'd tempt her toward the kind of destructive fantasies she'd made it her life's mission to avoid.

Nope. Whatever freaky mojo he'd been working back in Vegas wasn't in play today.

Not even a little.

Well fine, maybe a little.

There'd been an instant when Jeff opened his office door and she'd seen something hot in his eyes—but that was before she'd lunged past him making a practiced grab for the nearest garbage. Before the horror replaced the heat. And all the walls she'd suspected were there from the start slammed into place.

Now not even a little.

Which was good. Because her plate was more than full enough with this serving-for-two fate had dished her without having to worry about some weird chemistry snaking through the air between them. It distracted her with a momentary feel-good buzz she was too much of a realist to think might actually last, when she needed to focus on working out the details that would impact not just the rest of her life, but her child's, as well.

Their child's.

Her frenetic brushing slowed and she spit the paste.

God, what was he going to want? The mess cleaning reference didn't exactly suggest an instant, joyfully embraced, paternal connection. And how she felt about that... she didn't know.

On the one hand, her child would be lucky to have the kind of emotional security afforded by two parents who wanted it. But on the other, did either she or her baby really need to be tied to some overgrown kid who, by all appearances, didn't know the meaning of the word *no?* The man had made a desk of some repurposed airplane wing and a conference table from a disassembled jukebox topped in glass, for crying out loud. Essentially turning his workspace into a playground filled with the toys of a boy's heart.

And, yes, that boyish, world-on-a-string mentality packaged within a rugged all-man's body may have held some appeal when she first encountered it in Vegas. He'd known how to laugh. How to grab life with both hands and live in the moment without overanalyzing every move he made, without weighing every decision. And for a few incredible hours he'd shown her how to do the same.

But now, as that same mentality applied to the father of her child and with her body as exhibit A as one of the consequences to that *just for fun* mindset?

She let out a slow breath. Reached for the mouthwash, went for a bracing swish and spit.

Not so much.

Darcy placed a hand over her still flat belly, her emotions caught in a tug-of-war between awe over the precious life within her and resentment directed at herself. Disappointment. Frustration.

She'd known better. She'd spent years saying no to every temptation, because she'd had no one to count on but herself. No net to fall back in. No desire to allow herself to be trapped the way her mother had been.

She'd always been so relentlessly careful.

So how was it, this time, this one night, *this guy*...she'd said yes?

CHAPTER TWO

Three months earlier...

AND HERE HE'D thought he might be bored.

Within the swank Vegas lounge, Jeff Norton folded his arms over the tabletop, leaning forward in what had turned out to be a ringside seat for the crash-and-burn All-Stars playing out before him as a table of guys tried to score on the leggy blonde who'd just served him his Scotch.

He couldn't believe the one kid was throwing her a line after the world-class freeze she'd laid on the last chump. And his *friends* were encouraging him. Forget that on the hot scale, this woman ranked so far out of the kid's league, they weren't even on the same planet, let alone page. But hadn't they seen her eyes? The flat, wholly uninviting, all-business expression leaving zero wiggle room for misinterpretation: not interested. Period.

Probably not. These guys had a just legal look about them, which, coupled with their collection of empties lined up like trophies on the table, and the frequent "Vegas, baby!" fist pumps suggested they hadn't made it past the admittedly dynamite body before their brains blew out.

Live and learn, boys.

Thirty seconds later, the kid was taking a round of conciliatory back slaps from his cohorts and Jeff was back to waiting for Connor. His best friend fresh off a broken engagement and the reason behind this "guys' weekend" in Sin City.

Where the hell was he anyway?

Checking his texts, Jeff cursed seeing it was going to be at least another hour.

Screw it. He wasn't interested in watching guys, age twenty-one to ninety-three line up to strike out while Connor wrapped his call with Hong Kong. Flagging another server, he handed her his still full drink then pulled out a few bills for the table.

He was halfway to the door when feminine laughter, rich and warm, spilled down the hall beside the bar. The full-bodied sound of it snared his senses and had him cranking his head around to catch a glimpse of the source.

He stopped dead, his eyes locking on the silky blond ponytail streaming over one shoulder. The legs. The hourglass curves, and finally the softest, warmest, twinkling gray eyes he'd ever seen, crinkled at the edges as *his cocktail waitress* peered up at the ceiling laughing at whatever it was the shorter, redheaded server adjusting her shoe had said.

Gone was that untouchable, unattainable, disinterested, cold set of attractive features. And in their place was this *woman*.

No way.

And no wonder she'd kept that laugh under wraps. She could barely make it across the lounge as it was without some bozo putting a move on her. If anyone saw her like this...

Well, hell, their thinking would probably follow the same as his.

How do I get her to laugh like that for me?

They'd never leave her alone.

The redhead sauntered deeper down the hall and the leggy blonde with the killer laugh straightened her apron and turned—pulling up short at the sight of Jeff standing there.

The warmth and light from her eyes blinked off as she schooled her features back into a mask of utter disinterest.

The one that probably would have been easier to take if it were utter contempt because at least then a guy would know he'd made her radar. Damn, she was good.

Yeah, Jeff wasn't going anywhere.

"Another Scotch when you get a minute," he said, flashing her a grin before starting back to his table.

It wasn't like he'd come to Vegas with some plan to score. He hadn't. Only now the part of him that couldn't resist a challenge, the part that got off on getting what no one else could have—the fastest time, the highest grade, the biggest trophy, the most successful company—that part wanted to stake a claim on the secret prize so effectively hidden away, he wouldn't have believed in its existence if he hadn't heard the seductive, tantalizing sound of it himself.

And as it happened, he had an hour to kill.

Whatever the deal was with the guy from table twelve, Darcy didn't have time for it.

To think she'd pegged him as harmless.

Not in general, no. He definitely had the whole devastating male magnetism thing happening with those roughed up looks and his buttoned-down suit. Every set of female eyes in the place and probably half the men had homed in on him the second he entered the bar. But he hadn't been on the make—and she'd clocked enough hours in this lounge over the past two years to be able to tell. So she hadn't paid him much mind. At least not until she turned around to find him watching her with some half-cocked gotcha grin, looking like he'd busted her with her hand in the cookie jar.

Because he'd caught her *laughing.*

Something she didn't let happen very often at work as it tended to give the male clientele the wrong idea about what kind of good time she might be interested in having.

But then, tonight of all nights, what did it really matter?

Leaning a hip against the bar, she waited for Mr. Not-So-Harmless-After-All at table twelve's fresh Scotch.

This was her last night on the job. Her last—she checked her watch and felt a surge of excitement—two hours. And then she was through.

Sheryl Crow echoed through her mind, singing about leaving Las Vegas, and it was all Darcy could do not to put a little swing in her step as she pushed off the bar. Two more hours of tables to turn, drinks to serve, tips to make. And then she'd move on to life's next adventure.

Though even as she thought it, the word seemed an off fit to the relentlessly conservative way she managed her life.

Adventure implied risks and unknowns. Challenges. Excitement. That wasn't exactly how Darcy rolled. She couldn't afford to. Not after the steep price she'd paid to ensure her independence. She knew the suffocating experience of being at the wrong man's mercy and she'd been willing to sacrifice her education to facilitate that escape. Drop out of high school and get the job that set her free.

She'd sworn never to allow herself to be in a position of dependence again, which meant she took care of herself. She played it safe. Stayed in control. Lived within her means. And if the cost inherent to a life that felt safe was adventure of the tall, watered-down variety? She'd gladly pay it.

Stopping at table twelve, she leveled him with a flat stare. "Your Scotch, sir. Anything else?"

His speculative look had her wondering what this guy's game was exactly.

And then his focus lowered to her mouth, causing an unfamiliar dip and roll deep in her belly. One she met with a stern frown because oh, no, she was *not* going to be tempted by this guy. No way.

"Relax, Darcy. I get it. Not interested. Couldn't be more clear if you were wearing it on a T-shirt like the table of bridesmaids over there."

Her gaze shifted to the three women and the corner and

her mouth twitched, making something in his gut fire up. Though just as quickly she had the impulse tamped down.

"I'm not hitting on you," he assured. "This is about filling some hang time. You're my temporary hobby."

A slender brow pushed up. "How's that."

"I like the smile I saw. And I want one of my own."

That smooth hip of hers rocked out to one side. "You want a smile? I'll save you the hassle." She flashed him a grin barely a step above the flat business she doled out to every Tom, Dick and Harry who rolled through her section and Jeff shook his head, giving in to his own more sincere version.

"Nice try. But you're not going to put me off with some cheap imitation. I've seen the real thing, and now I want one for myself. An honest to goodness, hard-earned, full tilt smile. Bonus for the laugh. And no pity grins, either."

She opened her mouth to say something—probably another dismissive shutdown, but then pulled her mouth to the side as she studied him.

"So you want to work for it?" she asked.

And hot damn, was she actually going along? "I'm not into easy."

Her eyes were definitely on his now. Engaged in a way almost as satisfying as her elusive smile had been.

"Look—"

"Jeff," he supplied, without trying to take her hand because touching her would probably get him slammed up against an impenetrable wall of "no" faster than he could blink.

"Look, Jeff, you're interesting. Which is a nice change from the norm. But I'm working so I can't really hang out and be your *hobby* or anything else."

"Not a problem. I know you've got to work. So on average, how much time do you think you allot each customer outside of taking their actual drink order? I mean for the niceties: *Hello, how's your day? Good, yours? Good, know what you want?* Etcetera, etcetera, etcetera…"

"Fifteen seconds."

Nice try. "I'm talking the chatty ones."

"Forty-five."

"And if they're ordering, you'll give them the time?"

As if sensing a trap, she answered hesitantly, "Yes."

"Great. I'd like to send an order of white chocolate martinis to the bridesmaids over there. But tell them it's from the manager or something, not me."

When she just stared at him, he stared back. "I think our forty-five seconds are up. I mean, unless you'd like to sit down. You're welcome to stay for a drink. Take a break."

"This is because you're bored?" she asked, those steely gray eyes narrowing on him in a way that said he had her focus completely.

Had he really said he wasn't into easy? Because this was shaping up to be just that…and there wasn't a single molecule in his body or thought in his head, not totally into where it was going.

Jeff shrugged, raising his Scotch before taking a swallow. "I like to keep busy."

CHAPTER THREE

"CONSIDER IT A public service."

Darcy set the Scotch on a fresh napkin and, fighting her threatening smile with everything she had, slid it in front of Jeff. The guy who was making her last night in Vegas one she'd never forget. "Letting you take me out? Okay, let's hear it."

"Are you really going to make me say it?" he asked with a look all but begging her to make him do so.

She should walk away. She didn't date the customers and never gave into even this much interaction. But there was something about him. Something that wouldn't let her put him off the way she did with every other guy who crossed her path.

Even now, she could feel the corner of her mouth nearly betraying her as it threatened a smile. And Jeff knew it. He was watching, one brow raised. And then his eyes were locked back with hers. "Almost had you."

Yeah, it had been close.

"Okay, I give. How is my going out with you a public service?"

Satisfaction lit his smile.

"Because of my ego."

When she crossed her arms, he went on. "You've seen it. It's absurd. Honestly, the size is almost a handicap."

This was going to be good. Her brow pushed up, wanting more, but unwilling to open her mouth to ask for fear she'd break down laughing.

"If you crush this beast— Darcy, I'm not going to be able to drag it out of here."

"That big?"

"Like you really need to ask."

This guy was trouble. And exactly the kind of fun she deserved on her last night in Vegas. So long as it didn't go any further than a little flirtatious back-and-forth.

"I'm telling you, it'll be flailing around on the floor. Going boneless when I try to pick it up."

"Wow, almost like another person."

He offered a nod. "I call it Connor."

"An ego named Connor." Now she'd heard everything… and somehow it only made her want to hear more.

He let out a short laugh and rubbed a hand over his mouth as if trying to push the smile off his lips before going on. "And here's the problem. That ego's going to need some serious stroking to recover from your rejection."

Her eyes started to narrow, but he waved her off.

"It'll demand I hit on every female to cross my path. Forcing me to turn on the charm, we're talking full blast—"

"Like a fire hose?" she supplied, knowing she shouldn't have said it, but—well, she kind of couldn't help it.

Jeff's mouth was open, halfway to the next ridiculous part of his pitch when he froze. Cranked his eyes over to hers, the look in them one of amusement and warning.

"*Exactly* like a fire hose."

But for the way this guy was working her, there was something about him that seemed safe. Whatever it was, it was tempting her to push what she knew better than to play with. "So after you spray all these women down with your big hose. What happens then?"

"Widespread devastation. Women weeping everywhere. Broken hearts littering the streets. They're all going to fall in love with me, but all I'm really looking for is a date. Nothing serious. Just some fun."

Ahh, the circle back to her and suddenly eye contact

seemed more than she could handle. "And this is what happens every time a woman turns you down?"

Jeff shrugged, reaching for his Scotch. "Wouldn't know. It hasn't happened yet. Seriously, what kind of decent woman would want that kind of emotional carnage on her conscience?"

Darcy looked this guy up and down, taking in the details she'd glossed over before. The overly thick shock of dark hair with a mess of unruly cowlicks at total odds with the serious, straight cut of his classic suit.

But if the hair and suit were a working contradiction, they were nothing compared to his face. The heavy, squared-off jaw and single flashing dimple. The rough look of a nose that had seen a break or two and the ridiculously long fringe of dark lashes over eyes a soft, earthy hazel. On looks alone, this was a man who could keep a girl guessing. Add his confidence and charm to the mix and she imagined most women wouldn't mind playing Jeff's guessing game for as long as it was on offer.

Yeah, he was definitely more dangerous than she'd given him credit for.

Time to clear things up.

"Look, Jeff. I'm flattered, but I don't date customers. Ever."

"I noticed when I came in. I like it."

Mmm, and this she was definitely familiar with. "Because it makes me a challenge?"

"Yeah," he answered with an unrepentant grin and glint of mischief in his eyes.

And okay. Not so familiar after all. "Wow, and honest, too."

"It's the best policy. Eliminates the potential for all kinds of trouble. Ensures everyone is on the same page. But back to the issue at hand…I'm a fun date. You'd have a good time. There's got to be somewhere in town you've always wanted to go but haven't gotten around to. Tell me what it is and I'll take you tonight."

Darcy was about to shut him down, but as she stood there looking at that half-playful, too tempting smile all she could think was how many things she'd told herself she'd get to sometime, but never managed to do. And how long it had been since she'd really had fun.

Now her time was up. She was leaving tomorrow.

Jeff was offering her a chance to— God, was she seriously considering this?

She never said yes. Never gave in and did the fun thing for fun's sake. Maybe tonight, after living the straight and narrow for so very long, she could afford to break the rules without worrying about tomorrow.

"I'll think about it."

A few minutes later, Jeff was exchanging back claps with Connor Reed, whose call had been the typical success his buddy made of everything he set his mind to—the only glaring exception being a broken engagement from two weeks prior. One Connor wouldn't acknowledge any kind of emotional reaction to whatsoever. Hence, the *bromance* intervention in progress.

Because Jeff had been there. He knew what it was to be blindsided with the realization that the perfect romance you were about to bet your future on—not so perfect after all.

"No, I don't love him, Jeff. It's not about him. Or you. It's about me feeling trapped and doing something desperate to escape. I'm sorry."

Yeah, it sucked.

So, they'd done the gambling bit the night before, hit a few clubs and bonded in the manly way guys were most comfortable bonding. Thereby ensuring the whole guys' weekend spiel Jeff had lured Connor in with, wasn't a total snow job. But the grunts and knuckle bump portion of the weekend was at a close, and their friendship being what it was, Jeff made no bones about it.

Pushing the Scotch he'd ordered in front of Connor, he jut his chin at the drink. "You might want to get a head start on that."

Connor shot him the half smile he'd never quite figured out how to make whole. "Little old for drinking games, aren't we?"

"Time to put your big girl panties on, man. I brought you here to talk *feelings*. Deep emotional feelings. And because you know I'm your best friend *and always right,* you're going to sit there and take it like the man I know you can be."

The half smile was gone. "Jeff, I told you—"

"Don't bother. This is going to happen. But because I respect your stunted emotional intimacy boundaries, once I've said my piece we'll have a few minutes of smack talk, just to get back on comfortable ground and then I'm going to give you your space and take off. Most likely taking the blonde bombshell who happens to be our server with me. Deal?"

Connor picked up the glass in front of him and took a fortifying slug. Then cocking his jaw to the side, he leaned back in his chair and closed his eyes. "Okay. Let's have it. But make it fast."

Jeff caught Darcy watching him from over by the bar, a little furrow marring the otherwise flawless skin of her brow. He cast her a quick wink and then folded his arms over the table returning his attention to Connor.

"Your wish, my command. So, let me set the tone… I love you, man…."

A few dozen old adages, choice idioms, apt metaphors and select bits of fortune-cookie wisdom later, Jeff's work was done. There were things he'd needed the guy to hear, and things he needed to hear back. As it turned out, Connor hadn't been so bad off after all.

At least not in the way he'd imagined.

Emotionally stunted, however, didn't quite cover it as far

as the intimacy issues went. But that was a can of worms for another trip. Connor had given him his walking papers a few minutes ago and now Jeff leaned back against the bar, watching as Darcy worried her bottom lip.

No, she wasn't the unreachable, cold woman he thought at all.

"What about your friend? He looked really upset while you guys were talking."

Uncomfortable, yes. Upset, probably not. "Turns out the broken heart may have been more a case of dinged ego."

"You men and your egos. Does he name his, too?"

Jeff waved her in closer. "Guys don't tell other guys what they name their egos."

This time when he saw the little twitch at the corner of her mouth, he acted without thought and brought his thumb up to brush the vulnerable spot threatening to give him exactly what he'd been working for.

At the bare touch, her lips parted on a small gasp and their eyes met. Then quietly but firmly she said, "I won't go back to your room with you."

Jeff brushed that little corner of her mouth again and then withdrew his hand, parking it firmly in his pocket. "So when are we leaving?"

She searched his face as if looking for a reason to say no, and for one crushing instant when she ducked her head and glanced away, he thought he'd lost her. But she was just untying her apron. And when she looked back at him, it was with eyes that were confident, clear and determined. Excited. "As soon as I get out of this uniform."

"Does this count as sweeping you off your feet?" Jeff shouted, the laugh lines branching from his eyes, deeply creased, and the grin promising pure mayhem, gone full tilt.

"I'm totally carried away!" she gasped around the elated laughter she'd given herself over to.

The night breeze whipped at Darcy's hair as she careened

down to Freemont Street, gripping the security harness tight as she went and wondering if this rush of unadulterated exhilaration had more to do with the zip line or the man a few feet away.

Still decked out in his suit and rocking a very double-oh-seven vibe with the harness and wind and all, Jeff cocked his head in her direction. "Your turn to pick next, beautiful. I'm looking for some more local flavor. It better be good."

They'd been going back and forth for hours already, starting with a light dinner at one of the city's most coveted hot spots, where a twenty-second phone call from Jeff five minutes prior to their arrival scored them an immediate table complete with the VIP treatment and a breathtaking view. The restaurant had been her choice. One she'd only suggested because Jeff's cocky grin and wild assertion he could get them into any place she wanted to go had been a challenge she couldn't resist.

Turned out, there was more to the guy than talk.

Dinner, despite the upscale locale, had been casual and easy. The conversation varied and entertaining. Jeff was one of those men who seemed to know something about everything, and—whether the topic be movies, her wish list of travel destinations or the local economy—listened as much as he talked. And by the time they'd finished their coffees, Darcy had stopped second-guessing whether agreeing to go out with him had been a mistake, and was looking forward to finding out where they would go next.

From there they'd hit a rooftop roller coaster, stopped to get Jeff a snack at her favorite taco stand, driven out to the Neon Museum where the old signs of casinos past were put out to pasture, stopped to watch the choreographed fountains and then went on to walk the famous casino and hotel's gallery of fine art.

Along the way, Jeff seemed to make fast friends with everyone. He checked the score for big games with valets, and made small talk with old ladies when he held the door for them. He was the kind of smooth that normally had warning bells clanging in Darcy's head but for some reason, with Jeff, none of her typical knee-jerk reactions or default defenses were coming to the fore. In fact, she found herself letting go around him in a way she seldom did.

And the laugh he'd been working so hard to earn…well, once they'd left the casino, she'd given up the fight and had been paying with interest ever since. Laughing at his outrageous stories, at herself, at a last night in Sin City she never would have expected. A night she doubted she'd ever forget. Because not only was she experiencing a side of Vegas that had been previously unavailable to her, but thanks to Jeff's curiosity about her tastes, she had a last opportunity to relish those old favorites, by introducing them to him and explaining what made each a standout on her list.

It was a getting-to-know-you game. One she never would have played if she hadn't been leaving. But there was a safety in knowing this was just one night. No risk of expectations getting away from her. Darcy knew the score. This was about a few hours of fun. It was safe.

At least that's what she'd thought until the zip line ended and her feet touched the ground. Jeff walked over and, catching her hand in his, pulled her gently against him in a hold that really shouldn't have come across as anything but casual. Only with the heat of his body seeping into hers, the steady, deep thud of his heart beneath her hand and the warm rush of his breath teasing through the hair behind her ear as he asked in that low rough voice of his if she was having a good time—casual had never felt so intimate.

Tipping her head back to meet his eyes, she nodded, swallowing past a wordless reaction she wasn't accustomed to. A displaced sort of tug low in her belly made her feel as though she were flying and falling all at once. Jeff's gaze searched her own, drifted lower. Her thoughts went to the moment when he'd touched her mouth back at the bar. To the words she'd said.

...I won't go back to your room...

And the question of whether she still meant them.

"Let's go find someplace to get a drink and figure out what's next on our agenda," he said taking a step back as he let her go. The move was so unexpected, Darcy nearly stumbled at the absence of contact.

For an instant she'd been sure he would kiss her. Even now as he scanned the surrounding area in search of their next stop, she couldn't believe she hadn't felt the press of his lips against hers.

More, she couldn't believe she'd wanted to. Because what kind of madness would that be?

Jeff reached around her, resting his hand at the small of her back and asked, "What's the best bar in a three-block radius?"

The light contact felt good, even if for a crazy moment she'd thought she might want more. This was quality date stuff and she wasn't in any hurry to lose it. But a bar... "How about ice cream? There's a creamery just up the way here."

At Jeff's speculative look, she answered his unspoken question. "It's sort of a trust thing."

There was no judgment in his eyes when he asked, "You don't trust me? Or, and since you serve drinks for a living, I'm going to guess this isn't it, you don't trust yourself to stop?"

She laughed, leading the way as they walked. "The *only* person I trust is me. So don't take it personally. I like to stay sharp because I don't want to find out the hard way who I can or can't trust not to take advantage."

The easy smile Jeff had been sporting throughout the night slid from his lips and something dark and protective pushed into his eyes.

"Don't look at me like that," she said with a knowing shake of her head. "There's no horror story. At least not mine. In Vegas or probably any city, you hear things. I pay attention. And I'm just very…practical. I've always been like this."

Jeff's expression relaxed. "So you're risk adverse."

"Some would say to a fault."

"But not you?"

"But not me. If I thought I was doing something wrong, living in a way that didn't satisfy me or left me feeling like I was somehow missing out—I'd change it. Like I said, I'm pretty good at looking out for myself. I'm my number one priority. So I'm not really one to sit idle waiting for someone else to call out my problems or fix them for me."

"So you're a risk adverse woman of action, taking charge of your own destiny."

The corners of her mouth curled beneath his succinct categorization of her.

She'd been called a lot of things, by a lot of guys when they hadn't gotten their way with her. Cold, hard, icy. Names that indicated her lack of interest must stem from a short-coming on her part rather than a simple lack of desire to pursue something with a guy making passes at her while she was at work.

She slanted Jeff a sidelong look. He was just that—a guy making passes at her while she was working. And yet something about him struck her as so wholly different. Different enough, that as she kept telling herself the reason she'd agreed to go with him was because it was her last night in Las Vegas, some small part of her wondered if she would have gone with him whether she'd been leaving or not.

No. She shook the thought off, casting an inward scowl at the idea she'd do something that went against her principles after she'd just explained how keen she was on self-preservation.

"Strong and independent. A woman who knows her own mind. I like that."

"Yeah?" she asked, turning around to walk backward as she looked at him. "And me?"

"I definitely like you." He raked those big hands through the mess of his hair as he scanned the sky above them and then met her eyes with a straightforward stare. "I like the way you surprise me. That I didn't have you figured out within thirty seconds, or hell, even now, hours later."

Her steps slowed and Jeff closed the distance between them, resting his hand over the curve of her hip. "And I like that I can make you laugh, because the sound of it—"

He shook his head, still holding her gaze. "When you give into it for me—" his fingers tightened against her hips in a brief possessive grip "—all I can think about is how I'm going to get you to do it again."

"Jeff."

If he'd thought her laugh knocked him flat, hell, it was nothing compared to the breathy sound of her voice when she said his name like that. Like maybe she wanted the very thing he'd been about killing himself not to press for.

Sure once he'd made up his mind about getting her to go out with him back at the lounge, he'd assumed the natural progression of the evening would lead to a physical conclusion. They were both adults and there'd been a chemistry between them.

And he wanted it.

Hell, yeah, he did.

But something kept holding him back through each of those crossroad moments where the opportunity to change the tone of the night presented itself. The conflict in her eyes was like none he'd seen before. And it spurred some deeply instinctual need in him to protect her.

This woman he'd thought had ice in her veins and could level a man with one look alone was vulnerable and for some reason, tonight, she'd trusted him to take her out, show her the good time she all too rarely got and give her the night she deserved without whatever had her worrying that lush bottom lip of hers between her teeth. They could be the simple, uncomplicated, good time the other remembered in the years to come.

He smiled, thinking Darcy would get a kick out of that bit of fire-hose-flexing ego.

Who the hell knew if she'd remember him next week, let alone next year. But he hoped she would. Because he'd remember her.

What was she doing, looking into this guy's eyes like she couldn't physically make herself look away.

She didn't make the reckless choice. Not ever.

She didn't give in to the feel-good moment.

She liked control. In her work, in her life, in her heart and mind.

But somehow Jeff with all his ego talk, comfort in his own skin, confidence in his actions…his going after anything and everything he wanted like it never occurred to him he couldn't have it, was tempting her to behavior she didn't indulge in.

Making her want something she knew she shouldn't take. The experience of surrendering to a feeling. The chemistry tingling across her skin, batting around in her belly and whispering temptations through her mind since the first moment their eyes locked, and she realized this guy had just seen something she didn't show to anyone. And he'd liked it.

Her belly knotted tight at the idea of stepping so far out of her comfort zone. She'd already made too many exceptions. Starting with the conversation at his table and ending with the two of them standing here looking into each other's eyes.

Because Jeff was like a desert mirage. The kind of fantasy that could drive a woman to lose herself in the futile hope of finding shelter within a cool oasis that was never really within her grasp in the first place. Jeff was here for a single night. A few hours of fun.

She couldn't afford to lose sight of that because her pride wouldn't allow her to be one of those women who pinned all their hopes on the wealthy, jet-setting billionaire realizing the "good time" he picked up in Vegas—the city whose tourist industry had made a slogan of the promise that what happened in Vegas stayed in Vegas—was actually the woman he'd been waiting for his whole life.

No. The only way she could give in on any level, was if it was on her terms. With her eyes open and her expectations clear.

There was no tomorrow with this man.

"A lot of questions in those eyes tonight, Darcy." Jeff said, brushing her cheek with a single knuckle. "But there doesn't have to be. Tell me you're ready to call it a night and I'll take you home and thank you for an evening I won't soon forget. Or we can keep doing what we've been doing, without taking it any further at all. Stay up until morning. Watch the sun rise."

His eyes held hers as he asked, "What would you like to do next?"

Her heart raced. He was giving her a clear out. The easy goodbye.

She could tell him good-night. Take a cab home to her packed-up apartment. Sleep snug in the knowledge she'd cut things off before they'd gone too far. Before she gave in to the risks that pushed her beyond the boundaries of safe.

Or she could answer with the truth. That something about being with him made her ache for things she never wanted. Made her body shiver and heat. And most of all, want to grab hold of this moment and just give in to it. Surrender.

She reached for the open neck of his shirt and, letting two fingers curve into the gap between the button and plain white T-shirt beneath, pushed to her toes to meet his mouth with her own.

It was the barest of kisses. The lightest brush. Separated from a friendly peck only by a quiet, lingering beat promising what she hadn't found the words to say. Words she didn't need, based on the satisfaction in the eyes meeting hers as she stepped back into her own space. The wolfish smile as Jeff shook his head and, taking her hand, tugged her back against him.

"I've been telling myself no all night, Darcy," he murmured gruffly into her ear, rubbing his cheek against her hair. "If you're saying yes, that little kiss isn't going to be enough to tide me over until we get back to my room."

Her words were barely more than a trembling whisper. "Then you better take what you need now."

When he kissed her again, there was nothing tentative about it. Nothing friendly. It was firm and commanding. A decadent back-and-forth press of his lips against her own, deepening with every pass until she'd opened to him completely.

He licked into her mouth, his tongue gliding over hers in a wet velvet rub that had her fingers tightening in his shirt and a helpless whimper betraying her desire.

Her knees must have given out because he was holding her against him, supporting her in his powerful arms as he kissed her like she'd never been kissed before.

Senseless.

Breathless.

Taking her with the firm thrust of his tongue and—oh, that was so good—then again and again, until every part of her turned liquid and hot.

Needy.

Alive.

Another deep thrust and her belly twisted with a sensual hunger threatening to make her its slave. She'd been starved for this.

Jeff's arms snaked tight around her, one hand running the length of her back until it covered her bottom, firmed over her, pulled her in closer as he bent her back so she could feel him against her, and oh, yes, yes—

Abruptly Jeff broke from the kiss, setting her back a step even as he continued to support her. No!

"That was enough?" she asked, panting, her lips tender in a way that made her desperate for more.

"Not even close." He rubbed a hand over his mouth, the look on his face one of pure bewilderment. "But based on that kiss, I don't think either one of us wants to risk what will happen if I get my hands on you in public again."

Darcy wasn't so sure. For more of what she'd just had, she might be willing to risk anything.

CHAPTER FOUR

SOMEHOW THEY'D MADE it back to Jeff's suite. Barely. And when the door snicked closed, it was with Darcy against it. Jeff's hands braced above her head as he devoured the lush mouth he'd gotten only the cruelest taste of back on the strip.

She was so hot and wet and soft, and how they made it back without him pulling her across his lap in the cab or taking her against one of those mirrored walls in the elevator, he had no idea. Because once he saw the indecision gone from her eyes, and got his first taste of the heat she'd been keeping as much a secret as everything else—God help him, all he could think was *more.*

He rocked into her, nearly losing it at the sound of those desperate little noises she kept making. The humming and moaning. Catching her breath when he hiked her legs at either side of his hips and ground against her. Purring when, after she locked her ankles at his back and urged him on, he did it again and again and again—driving them both mad with the contact that wouldn't be enough until the clothes were gone and he was thrusting hard and deep inside her.

"Jeff, please," she whimpered against his jaw, her body taut as he pushed her closer toward the peak she'd be visiting about a half dozen times over the next few hours if he had his way.

"Like this, baby?" he asked, canting his hips so the hard shaft of his erection rolled over her sweet spot.

Another desperate cry and her fingers knotted in his hair.

He'd take that as a yes.

"Jeff!" she gasped a second before her body arched and her lips parted on a silent cry that held and held and held but never found its voice. One that invited him to take advantage, licking and nipping as he carried her through the last waves of pleasure. And then she was kissing him back, her lax body a satisfying contrast to his. Her eyes, heavy-lidded and soft like he hadn't seen them yet.

So gorgeous.

So damn sweet.

And for tonight, his.

Though even as he thought it, he realized one night wouldn't be enough. Hell, he'd known before she kissed him he'd be back.

"Darcy," he started, his mouth moving against the slender column of her neck. "This, tonight—"

Her fingers tightened in his hair as she urged him back to her mouth. "I know. It's perfect. Everything I didn't think I wanted."

She kissed him again, distracting him with the slide of her tongue playing over his and the wiggle of her hips as she unlocked her ankles and went back to her feet. Her delicate hand smoothing down the front of his shirt, over his chest and stomach, and down the jutting ridge of his erection still contained behind the confines of his suit pants. He pushed into her palm, groaning at the feel of her stroking him through the fabric and then curling her fingers into his belt and, walking backward, tugged him toward the bedroom.

Perfect.

It was the single thought in his head, reverberating with each step as he let her lead him toward the only salvation he wanted.

They pulled at each other's clothes, reveling in each new stretch of bared skin, tumbling onto the bed in a frenzied, desperate tangle of limbs. Darcy grabbed the condom he'd tossed up by the pillow and tore open the foil.

"I can't wait," she panted, her hands trembling as she began rolling the latex down his more than ready shaft.

"No more waiting," he agreed, positioning himself between her legs so he was notched at her slick opening.

Their eyes met, and he pushed inside her with the first shallow thrust. It nearly killed him to pull back, but he wasn't a small man and Darcy—heaven help him, she was so very tight. So he went slowly, carefully, penetrating by degrees until sweat beaded over his brow and his jaw clenched and finally he took her the way he needed to. Completely.

And then he was sliding full-length in and out of Darcy's tight, wet heat, letting her soft moans and broken breath lead him down the decadent path to her pleasure, answering the needy clutch of her body when he touched her just right, reveling in the helpless surrender of her eyes when he held her at the brink—

"Tell me what you want."

"Please, Jeff," she gasped, her heels digging at the back of his thigh as she urged him toward the contact he wouldn't give her until she gave him what he wanted first.

"Say it. Tell me and I'll give you anything."

Looking into his eyes, she gave up her fight for control, let her knees slide farther up his ribs and whispered, "Make me come."

And then firmly he pushed her into oblivion…making sure not to follow himself. He wasn't close to done with this woman.

Breathless. Boneless. Stunned and sated, Darcy lay within the damp sheets blinking at the ceiling as her body and mind worked in frantic concert to pull all the shattered bits of her back into some semblance of their previous working order. This wasn't the way she was supposed to feel. Like something monumental had occurred. Like there'd been a sudden unexpected shift in her life. Like she'd had her first taste of *incredible* and from that point forward, nothing again would compare.

Because this was a one-night stand.

A date gone past midnight with a man who most definitely wasn't her Prince Charming.

It was a one-off.

A last fling, because Jeff might be gorgeous, fun and devastating in bed…but he wasn't offering her more than a good time.

They'd spent hours laughing and talking and working up to this last brash act, and for all the chemistry between them, for each glint in his eye that told her he was having as much fun as she was, there was another opportunity left untaken when he might have suggested the possibility of more. Asked about another date. Implied he was even considering something beyond a single night of simply killing time together.

The man was smooth. Slick. And just because he had the ability to make *her* act out of character didn't mean tonight was anything out of the norm for him. For all she knew, Jeff hit a new bar each week, making his Friday night special the most hard-to-get girl in the place.

"Darcy, Darcy, Darcy." Her name, rumbling against her neck like pebbled kisses, pushed all thoughts from her mind but one. It didn't matter what Jeff did every other Friday night. This one he'd shared with her had been perfect.

Jeff lifted his head, pushing up on his arms to ease the weight of his body over hers—a weight she hadn't been ready to give up and felt the immediate loss of as cool air slipped between the growing space between them.

Backing off the bed, he got sidetracked by her breast, which he stopped to kiss once at the side, then again on her nipple before casting her a wicked grin as he finished his retreat. "Give me a minute, sweetheart. Don't go anywhere."

She watched him walk to the bathroom and close the door behind him. Heard the muffled sound of the running tap and waited as the seconds ticked past.

Alone in the bed, she glanced around at the suite, noting the luxurious accommodations for the first time. It seemed extravagant. Frivolous.

Sure it wasn't like he had sixteen rooms, but a suite, for one man through two nights?

The moments stretched by. The water was still running.

Beginning to feel somewhat self-conscious she reached for the sheet at the side of the bed, but came back with a handful of blouse instead.

Don't go anywhere...

She looked at the sliver of light breaking beneath the door and then at the shirt in her grasp.

Don't go anywhere...

Five minutes ago she wouldn't even have considered it. She would have flopped back on the bed relishing the full-body fatigue that was the result of Jeff's thorough attention.

Obviously, she wouldn't have planned to stay forever. But she wouldn't have considered up and leaving while he was in the other room, either.

Except then he'd gone and said it, and a thousand and one thoughts started pushing into her mind. They'd had sex. It was over. And though Jeff might not want her to run off that second, it was obvious from his words he expected her to go shortly. Which made perfect sense, this being what it was. A little meaningless fun.

But as she sat in the middle of his big bed, the heat of their intimacy dissipated into the air around her, what had happened between them still fresh and tender in her mind—so good—she wanted to protect the memory of it. This night had been a gift to herself. And she didn't want to risk the simple perfection of it being lessened by Jeff's inevitable dismissal.

Chances were, he'd be as adept at a goodbye as he'd been with everything else. And yet rather than wait, she found herself pulling on her shirt. Dragging the sheet off the bed with her as she sifted through the blast radius of discarded clothing, darting glances at the bathroom door as the water continued to run.

She didn't want to be the one clinging to their last minute together. The one waiting to be excused.

She'd known what she was getting with Jeff from the start. A few hours of fun. He'd made sure she understood back at the bar.

Another look at the clock.

It's why he'd chosen her in the first place. Because he'd recognized she had the sense not to get ideas where they didn't belong.

Jeff gripped the marble countertop, staring at his reflection as he tried pull himself together and figure out what to say.

Damn it, he *always* knew what to say. But he'd been off his game since about minute one with Darcy. Closing his mouth around a tongue inexplicably tied up over a girl he couldn't quite figure out. And hadn't had nearly enough of.

That's where his head had been when he dragged himself out of bed, walked into the bathroom with the intent to clean up and then come back with an offer of...*something*.

Something more than the cursory "thanks for the great time, have a nice life" that generally came as standard with the kind of night they'd just indulged in.

He liked her. Liked the way she made him laugh and her unique perspective on—well, hell—everything. Sure she lived in Vegas, and this wasn't exactly a typical stopover for him. But if she was receptive, he'd been thinking about making it one. Or better yet, swinging by to pick her up and bring her down to L.A. once in a while. For an overnight or maybe even a weekend.

That's where his head had been until he looked down to discover the condom he'd been using had failed in a no-maybe-about-it kind of way.

Now? He was trying to figure out how to break the news to Darcy, rolling through the scenarios, imagining what he was going to see on her face when he told her. Accusation, fear, dread.

The idea he would cause her any of those things was like a blow to the gut. He wasn't *that guy.* Not to anyone.

Not after Margo, his girlfriend through most of high school and college, and the woman he'd assumed, like everyone else, he would marry. At least until the day she'd come to him red-eyed and blotchy-cheeked with the confession she'd slept with another guy. She'd felt claustrophobic, trapped by all the expectations of their too serious, too neat, too well-planned relationship. She'd wanted out and, though a phone call would have been less traumatic to all involved, she'd found her escape in the bed of some frat guy with a coke habit.

As a result of that lesson, Jeff had all but perfected the no-hold relationship. He was a safe guy. A good time. The lover who always remained a friend after, because the romance never went too deep to come back from.

He kept his finger on the pulse of his affairs, making communication a priority. It was why he'd gotten his reputation as "Mr. Sensitive"—which was fine by him if it meant avoiding another blindside like the one he'd taken with Margo. Hell, yes, he'd talk about feelings. And the added benefit of that open dialogue? Nothing got too serious. No one got the wrong idea.

He was *not* the guy who put panic into someone's eyes. But that's what was about to happen. Because if ever there was a way to make a woman feel trapped, this was it.

Pulling it together, he reminded himself while this was the first time it had happened to him, it certainly wasn't the first time a condom had broken in history. Both he and Darcy were adults who understood prophylactics weren't 100 percent. Accidents happened. And this was an accepted risk inherent to sex.

They'd talk. He'd assure her he was compulsive about using protection and he was clean. She'd tell him that while she didn't generally go home with guys she just met, she was on birth control and also clean. They'd exchange contact information and stay in touch.

But whatever fantasies Jeff had been entertaining about going forward with a casual relationship had pretty well shriveled under the icy splash of reality offered in the form of a blown-out rubber. And now all he was thinking was he'd be damn lucky to make a clean getaway.

Tightening the towel wrapped around his hips, he headed out of the bathroom and froze with one hand midrub at the back of his skull, his mouth open and all thoughts of what he'd been about to say gone—just like the woman he'd been inside of less than ten minutes before.

CHAPTER FIVE

Present day...

MOMENTS LATER THE bathroom door swung open and the mother of what was presumably his child emerged.

The cool steely gray of her eyes met with his. Eyes he remembered warming through the course of those hours they spent together. Eyes he'd watched go soft beneath him, and had made him wonder if a single night was going to be enough. Eyes that had haunted him for weeks after he'd been back in L.A., until he'd forced himself to put them out of his head. Get a new game plan and move on.

Which is exactly what he'd done.

Olivia.

Pinching the bridge of his nose, he gave his head a stern shake. *One thing at a time.*

Darcy took a nervous breath and then cleared her throat. "So, maybe we should start by getting a few things straight up front."

Jeff nodded, checking the legal pad he'd started making a list on. "Agreed."

Validate paternity.
Confirm/upgrade health care.
Establish child support.
Hire nurse.
Buy house with yard and security.

Start screening for nanny.
Private preschools (*gifted and talented programs?).
Top five universities in country.
Quality playgroups.
Safety reports *family vehicles.

"I don't want to marry you," she said abruptly, wincing almost as soon as the words left her mouth.

Jeff blinked.

Wait. *She* didn't want to marry *him?*

He blew out a measured breath while mentally talking his ego down from the ledge. Because seriously, after slinking out of his bed without so much as a "thanks for the good time, sport," *that's* how she wanted to kick this conversation off?

"Not that I remember asking," he said evenly. "But good to know we're on the same page."

Or maybe not quite so evenly after all, considering the slender brow arched in his direction, topping off an all too familiar look that did something to him not entirely bad, but not exactly welcome, either.

Their eyes held a beat before she glanced away. "And I'm not interested in picking things up where we left off."

"Something the woman I'm seeing will appreciate, I'm sure."

Yeah, and best to get that out there right away, even though he was fairly certain there wasn't one thing about this Olivia was going to appreciate.

Especially if she ever got a look at Darcy. Because even having just spent twenty minutes losing her lunch, she was still a knockout. So far as he could see the pregnancy hadn't done much to her body yet.

Before he realized where that thought was taking him, his attention was doing a slow crawl south of her neckline, roaming over the full curves and narrowing tucks of a figure that—

"That's great about your girlfriend, but I'm not here to option my baby, either, so…" Her fingers came into his line of sight which happened to have stalled out around the navel he'd dipped his tongue into, snapping twice and then veering into the universal *eyes up here mister* flag. "…so whatever you're thinking with that look on your face? Stop."

"*Optioning* your baby?" he choked out. "Excuse me?"

Her shoulders squared up.

"Well, you were staring," she shot back with an accusing jut of her chin. Then seeming to lose a bit of her bravado, she more quietly added, "With a sort of greedy, speculative look on your face. How am I supposed to know what you're thinking?"

Jeff shook his head, opened his mouth once and then simply closed it again, because…

Really?

And then it was like the tension that had been accumulating since she'd first lunged past him…just snapped. And suddenly, all he could do was laugh. Which probably didn't do much to alleviate the whole greedy, speculative vibe he'd been putting off, but oh, well. Apparently there wasn't much lower he could sink to in Darcy's eyes.

So instead, he simply rubbed his palms over his cheeks and looked across at the woman who'd turned his life upside down in a single night, and just when he thought he'd put it back to rights, showed up and sent him into a tailspin.

One he needed to pull out of and fast.

"Relax. I got distracted by your body. It doesn't look like it's changed much." And at the risk of coming across like a jerk, he added the truth. "You look good, Darcy."

"Oh." Then after a moment she rolled her eyes as if making some painful, grudging acknowledgment herself. "Thank you. You look good, too. Even though it doesn't matter."

He couldn't help the grin, but as it turned out, she didn't seem to mind, answering with one of her own.

It caught him off guard, but he recovered quickly, suggesting they sit down and talk.

Darcy stepped away from the door and crossed over to the couch where Jeff set an empty can on the floor, out of the way but still within reach.

She looked down and her eyes fluttered through a few wet blinks. "You got a fresh can for me?"

She was looking at him like he'd just handed over the keys to a new Mercedes.

"I didn't want you to have to put your face in the old one."

Her hand moved to what was still the flat plane of her belly and she gave him a watery half smile he didn't quite understand, but sensed meant something important to her. "You're a thoughtful guy, Jeff."

And there it was. Reassurance. Because she had to be scared out of her mind right now, coming to him when he was virtually a stranger.

Reaching for her hand, Jeff gave it a brief squeeze and looked her in the eyes. "Hey, this is all going to work out fine. Don't be nervous." He sat back, legal pad in hand. "So, where should we start—after, you're pregnant, of course."

She winced almost as if hearing the words was still new and shocking to her. But then maybe that was the best place. "When did you find out?"

"I didn't know until a week ago. Which is late, but…" She offered a frustrated little shrug. "My cycle is irregular enough so I don't really wait around for it and, normally I don't have any reason to anyway. But the past few months… I've been running pretty much nonstop. I thought the stomach upset was nerves. Then it got worse and I thought I must have caught the flu everyone was talking about, except it didn't get better."

He was following her words, but a part of him was still stuck on this news being nearly as new to Darcy as it was to him. "Have you been to a doctor yet?"

"For the blood test." She opened her purse, retrieved the

printout she'd gotten from the lab and handed it over. "But my first appointment isn't until next week."

Jeff scanned the paperwork before setting it on the small table beside his chair. "So, if you don't want to get married, or pick things up from where we left off...I think it makes sense to ask, what do you want?"

"I'd like you to agree to a paternity test."

Darcy could see the wheels turning in his head, the man stepping back from the prospect of fatherhood with the idea maybe this child wasn't his.

"Jeff," she said as gently as she could. "You should understand, I'm only asking for the test for your benefit because I don't expect you to take the word of some woman you knew for a handful of hours three months ago. But there are no other options. This baby *is* yours. Once you have the confirmation from a lab, the decision you need to make is whether you want to be a father to it. That's what I need to find out."

Jeff was watching her closely, his eyes so intense she had to fight the urge to squirm under his scrutiny. For a guy who could do irreverent like she'd never seen it done before, there was another, more serious, side to Jeff to balance it. And in this moment, the balance was a comfort.

"No other *options?* You're telling me you haven't slept with anyone else since we were together."

She took a bracing breath, not insulted by his request for clarification. "I realize I haven't given you much reason to believe this, but I don't make a habit of going home with guys I just met. Or at all, really. There wasn't anyone else."

Jeff drew a long slow breath, his eyes still on her, but his focus seemingly directed inward. He nodded.

"Okay. So the test is basically a formality. I'll have Legal look into it and set something up. In the meantime, I'm going to be a father. I may need to get used to the idea, but as to whether I'm up to the responsibility, there's no deliberation necessary." He pushed to his feet and walked back to his desk. "So how are we going to do this?"

"Could we start with the paternity test and go from there?" she asked. "This is still so new to me, too. I wanted to get in touch with you right away, but I haven't worked out exactly how *I feel* about everything. I guess I just wanted to know where you stood before I started making too many decisions about a future you might want a say in."

He let out a contemplative breath. "Okay. I can respect that. And I appreciate it. So we'll take this one step at a time. Start with the test. You could think about whether moving is something you'd consider and we'll set something up to talk in a week?"

She nodded, relieved by his easy accommodation and perhaps by the distance he'd established between them with that last parting comment. It would be an appointment. Because they were going to handle this like business.

Exactly the way she wanted them to.

CHAPTER SIX

WITH HIS AFTERNOON cleared, there was nothing Jeff would have rather done than call Connor. Tell his best friend he wasn't the only one to pick up a souvenir in Vegas. Talk out the changes ahead of him and have the guy—the only guy on the planet who knew him as well as he knew himself—tell him he had his back.

But Connor had just reconciled with his wife—a woman he'd married within hours of meeting that same night Jeff met Darcy—and even if Jeff thought he could live with himself for interrupting them…he was fairly certain the two lovebirds were still off the grid.

Just as well.

There was someone else who deserved to know what was happening first.

Olivia. The woman he'd started a relationship with five weeks ago. The *something* Jeff had found to fill the empty spot in his life he'd only become aware of after Vegas.

Jogging across the marble-and-glass atrium, Jeff caught the elevator to Olivia's top floor office.

How the hell was he going to explain this? And how would she take it?

Things had been going well with them. They'd been a smart fit from the start. Comfortable together, compatible.

She was open and pleasant. Harvard educated. Business savvy. Connected.

Two hours ago, he would have given it six months at the outside before he popped the question. And only because it seemed like an appropriate time to wait. In Olivia he'd found a woman who was all the things he'd known he wanted for a partner in life from as far back as he could remember— from the first time he looked across the table at his parents and thought to himself, *someday, I want that.*

The business journal over morning coffee. The dinners at the club. The shared interests for their shared lifestyle. The sparkling hostess championing the charities and foundations they supported.

It sounded shallow as he itemized it in his head, but it wasn't.

He wanted the kind of good match that meant a lifetime of companionable, easy happiness. What his parents had up until the day five years ago when a heart attack took his father. The best man he'd ever know. The example Jeff had always hoped to live up to. Hell, he wished he was around to talk to about this.

Riding up to Olivia's, he couldn't help question what she would think when she looked at the woman he'd been with before her. The one who'd been his wake-up call about putting an end to the screwing around with women who weren't right for him and thinking about getting serious with one who was. Settling down. Starting a family.

Olivia would see everything she wasn't when she looked at Darcy.

And it would make her wonder.

Darcy had been a good time he hadn't seen coming. And the only reason she'd gotten under his skin the way she had was because of the way she'd left.

So the chemistry between them had been hot enough that even months later, he could feel the lingering burn of it, so what? That was sex. Not exactly a foundation to build a solid forever on. But neither was it something he could, in good conscience, ignore when it came to a relationship with another woman.

"Hey, Mel. She in?" he asked, when he got to her office.

"She's on a call. Should I interrupt?"

"No. I'll wait."

This was news he needed to tell her today and in person.

Sometime later, Jeff was searching stages of pregnancy on his phone, checking them against his calendar and travel commitments when Olivia's office door swung open and she walked out to greet him with a welcoming smile.

"Jeffrey, what a wonderful surprise!"

"Got a few minutes for me?" he asked, unfolding from the deep sofa to lead her back into the office. And once there, he closed the door behind them. "Is it private in here?"

Olivia's brow crumpled a bit at the question as she looked at the closed door behind him and then her neatly organized desk loaded with her current projects. "I was thinking you might be here to take me to lunch." Her nose crinkled before reluctantly meeting his eyes again. "But are you here for something…else?"

A bark of laughter escaped him as he realized the direction of her thoughts. She'd thought he was here for some kind of afternoon desktop quickie. Yeah, now he got her confusion. It wasn't exactly like that between them.

Shaking his head, he crossed to the cluster of club chairs across her office and held a hand out asking her to join him. "No, Olivia, I'm sorry. Something…unexpected has come up. We need to talk."

A little furrow had cut between her delicate brows as she lowered herself into the chair across from him. "You're worrying me, Jeffrey. What's happened?"

Looking at her guileless face and earnest eyes, he wished there was some way to sugarcoat the bitter news he was about to give her. But it wouldn't help either of them. "A couple of months before we met, I spent the night with a woman who came to my office today. She's pregnant."

Olivia sat stone still, her eyes gone wide. "Was there something between you?"

He opened his mouth to say no, but said instead, "It was one night."

"Who is she? Would I know her? Is she the type to keep quiet? What does she want from you?"

"I doubt very much you know her, unless you've spent more time in Vegas than you let on."

"She's a *stripper.* Oh, God, Jeffrey, please tell me she isn't a prostitute."

"No!" He raked a hand back through his hair. "No, she was the waitress at a bar I was stuck at waiting for Connor the night he met Megan. I was killing time and one thing led to another."

He didn't like the sound of his explanation, but the deeper, expanded version of the truth wasn't something Olivia needed to hear.

"You just found out? So, there hasn't been any time for conclusive paternity testing, then. This baby might not even be yours. I mean, Jeffrey, one night with some *Vegas cocktail girl* three months ago. We don't know anything yet."

A part of him wanted to agree. Tell her she was probably right and to give him a few weeks to sort it out. Only she deserved the whole truth. "We'll have the DNA testing done, but I already know this baby is mine."

She didn't ask for details but he could see the understanding in her eyes. The way the hope shifted toward disappointment.

She swallowed, withdrawing her hands from his to tuck them around her waist. "Are you going to marry her?"

Darcy's emphatic pre-proposal rejection came to mind, pushing a wry smile to his mouth. "No."

"Okay," she said, nodding slowly before meeting his eyes with a steel he hadn't encountered in hers before. "Then cut her a check."

He stared hard at the woman seated across from him, the one he'd thought might be able to share his life. "To what, go away? Disappear?" He couldn't even voice the next alternative he hoped to hell she wasn't suggesting.

Something roared inside him, as a protective instinct churned hot in his gut. "It's *my child.*"

"And we'll raise it as ours," she said quickly, taking his hands. "We'll get married. Have a private adoption. We'll craft an explanation to suit us both."

Adoption. Of course, that's where Olivia's head would have gone first. Adoption and marriage. A neat package, except for the part where she'd completely discounted Darcy as a part of the equation beyond a dollar amount on a check.

"Jeffrey, we have something here. Something I've been waiting to find for a very long time. We could make this work."

Offering Olivia's hand a quick squeeze, he pushed up from his chair.

He needed to cut Olivia some slack. She'd jumped to the wrong conclusion, probably because the few details he'd parceled out pointed that way. She was trying to come up with a solution to a problem he'd dropped in front of them. It just wasn't the right one.

Walking over to the bank of windows, he rubbed his hand over his jaw. Darcy was right. They all needed a little time to get their heads around this new development.

"Darcy doesn't want to give the baby up. She was offering me an opportunity to be a part of its life. Not to…option it off. You don't know her."

Olivia sat back, watching him the way he watched guys from across the conference table. Reading their tells and all the things their faces and bodies said without their mouths having to. "And you do?"

"Only enough to say, she wasn't here to give her child up."

"Okay. Then we'll take it from there." She followed him across the office, laying her hand gently over his arm.

"Olivia, I don't know what this next year is going to bring. I think it might be better for everyone if we—"

"No. I'm not going to give up on us because things aren't exactly the way I thought they would be." She met his eyes. "We're so well suited. So right. All I'm asking is you give us a chance before making any decisions. Please."

Jeff wrapped an arm around her shoulders. She felt stiff against him. Like an off fit in a way he'd never noticed before.

Which he supposed made sense, considering he'd just put something between them neither of them knew exactly how to deal with. Now the least he could do was grant her request and give them a chance.

CHAPTER SEVEN

"You got the *waitress* pregnant?" Connor shook his head, rocking back on his bar stool as though the news had physically blown him over. "You're sure? I mean, all the question marks...?"

Jeff nodded. "Had a DNA test pushed through, but even if I hadn't—I'm sure."

"A baby. How in the hell?"

At Jeff's raised brow, the other man held up a staying hand.

"Don't. I know how. Your dad did a bang-up job with the 'talk' back in high school. I just can't believe—you—like this—now." Then shooting him a concerned look, he asked, "Someone mentioned you were seeing Olivia Deveraux. That you two might be serious."

"Before Darcy showed up at my office, I would have put money on a future with Olivia. But now." Now, even two weeks later, he wasn't any closer to knowing what their future held. Olivia hadn't changed. "She wants it to work. Offered to marry me and adopt the baby."

"Generous."

"If Darcy were considering giving it up. But not for even a single second."

He thought about her busting him looking at her narrow waist, and accusing him of trying to option her baby. Once again giving in to the reoccurring grin that stomped all over his face every time he thought about her outraged, accusing look, he held up his hands. "She's going to be an amazing mother. You can see it."

"Olivia?"

Jeff caught Connor's stare and the subtle, unspoken question behind it. "*Darcy*. But, yeah, I'm sure Olivia would, too."

Connor pushed his drink around in a neat square on the bar. "But you don't *see it* with her?"

Worse, he wasn't even sure he'd looked. Olivia had asked him to give them a chance and so far he hadn't made the time to actually do it.

"I've been so focused on Darcy, there hasn't been a lot of time for anyone or anything else. She's living in San Francisco and I've been trying to talk her into moving down here. But she's...stubborn. I think she intends to move, but not until the baby comes. She's got a job and—" He shook his head. "And the job thing is a really big deal to her. But I'm not giving up. I want her here, like yesterday."

"Am I missing something about the waiting tables thing? What the hell kind of job does she have that *you* can't compete with it?"

Jeff rocked back in his chair and expelled a frustrated breath. "One she got for herself."

Understanding lit Connor's eyes. "She does know who you are, right?"

"She doesn't *care* who I am." He raked a hand through his hair. "She won't take any money until the baby comes. And, damn it, she's just very independent...and stubborn."

Connor's brows pulled together and his jaw cocked to one side.

Jeff scowled at him. "It's not like that. Even if Olivia weren't in the picture. We've already agreed, in no uncertain terms, neither of us is interested in picking things up from where we left them. What Darcy is to me is the most important person in the life of the most important person in mine. Our relationship is going to be about this kid and it's got to work forever. Which means there's too much at stake to risk any potential friction over some affair gone bad."

And he knew from experience what the fallout from a failed relationship could cost.

Connor took a swallow of his drink. "Right. Definitely not worth the risk for an affair."

Jeff stared at him. "I'm serious."

A nod. "Okay."

Oh, that burned. "Bite me."

Connor grinned and flagged the bartender for the tab. "Sorry, my friend. Megan doesn't share."

The elevator doors opened at the eleventh floor and Jeff followed Olivia down the hall toward her apartment.

She cast a bright smile over her shoulder at him, her efficient steps eating up the distance to her door. "Thank you for dinner tonight. I know how busy you've been."

That was Olivia. Not raking him over the coals. Sensitive to the situation he was in while letting him know she still enjoyed seeing him when the opportunity arose. He hadn't meant for their relationship to fall by the wayside, but he'd been neglecting her for weeks. Working long hours and even through the couple of times he'd taken her out, he'd been distracted. There, but not *really* there. Because being with Olivia wasn't enough to keep his mind from visiting all the places he didn't want it to go. To Darcy.

To the space he was trying to give her, and how hard he was trying not to hate the space she already had. To wondering what she'd do if he pushed too hard.

It wasn't fair. But Olivia had been so accommodating. Assuring him she understood. He shouldn't put her off. He shouldn't be able to.

And yet, as he walked behind her his mind kept drifting to another woman. How she was feeling? If anyone was making her laugh? If her belly was starting to show?

"You're coming in?" Olivia asked at her door, putting the

breaks on a train of thought threatening to go off the rails and pulling him back to the woman who ought to be holding his attention for the few hours they had together.

She was watching him expectantly. As if she knew, mentally he'd already dropped her at her door and was halfway back to the office. Where he'd have a fighting chance of losing himself in work.

"Olivia," he started, catching her chin in the crook of his finger. "I've got a call scheduled with Hong Kong in three hours."

She leaned a shoulder against the frame of the door and looked him over assessingly.

"Then you've got two and a half to spend with me." Her fingers wrapped around his tie to tug him closer. "I know you've been waiting, not pushing the physical element of our relationship out of respect for me, but it's time. You need a distraction, Jeff. Let me help you forget for a while."

Respect. Maybe that was part of what had been holding him back. But to really respect her meant acknowledging that not taking the next physical step in their relationship had been far too easy. She deserved better than to be used as a distraction. And far, far better than a distraction he already knew wouldn't work.

He'd tried to tell himself this was the woman for him. The perfect fit he'd imagined her to be when they first started seeing each other. Because she'd been so different from the one who'd walked away... But once Darcy stepped back into the picture he'd started making comparisons.

"Jeff, you said you'd give us a try. Can't you please, come in and let me show you how it could be between us, if you let it?"

He hated the pleading in her eyes, hated knowing it was about to turn to hurt. But it was, because his hands had already moved to her shoulders, gently putting the space back between them. "I'm sorry, Olivia."

Oh, no, not again.

Darcy sat at the folding table in the suddenly too warm

back room of the party coordinating business where she'd been hired to inventory catering supplies, stuff envelopes, assemble favors, scoop birdseed satchels and anything else the overbooked business needed assistance with during their seasonal rush.

The pay wasn't great, but she'd been lucky the manager of the restaurant where she'd been working had put in a good word with the owner to get her the temporary position. And at least she was maintaining an income, if somewhat reduced.

A few more weeks and the nausea would ease because it couldn't get any worse. And once her stomach was back under control—

As if on cue, her belly lurched again.

"You okay?" her boss asked from the open doorway.

Darcy pushed to her feet, lifting a hand to let the older woman know she was fine. Except the shrinking edges of the room hazing into sepia tones warned she wasn't.

She tried to get a hand back to the table, but too quickly everything went loose and dark and down until there was only one thought left in her head…and that was the silent plea that her baby be okay.

Darcy woke slowly, her senses coming back online one at a time as she registered the hard mattress of the hospital bed beneath her, the dimmed overhead light and the deep rumble of a voice she hadn't been expecting. One which shouldn't have been coming from anywhere near her.

Jeff.

"…Dehydration, fatigue, low blood pressure, weight loss… No, they say both she and the baby will be all right, but there's no way in hell I'm leaving without—"

She shifted in the bed, remembering too late about the needle threaded into her vein and letting out a short gasp when she put weight on it.

Whatever Jeff had been about to say, she missed and now

the conversation was over. Jeff was suddenly in her room, filling up the small space with his enormous presence. Dropping his phone into the inside pocket of his suit jacket, he crossed to her bed like he was going to slide into the open chair beside her. But instead, he reached for the call button and signaled the nurse before taking a step back. Fixing her with a serious look. "Do you need anything? How are you feeling?"

"Tired still, but, Jeff, you didn't need to come. I told Charlie, they just wanted me to get some fluids and an antinaus—"

"You told me *you were fine.*" It wasn't exactly accusation she was getting off him, but the intensity was like a palpable thing. "I spoke to your doctor already and *hyperemesis gravidarum* can be dangerous and severe. You are *not* fine, Darcy."

Guilt washed over her in a wave. She'd thought it was just morning sickness in an all-day, extended package, which she'd heard was normal, too. Though she'd planned to speak to her doctor at her next checkup about the extremity of it, she'd had no idea her body had begun turning against her, threatening what she'd been struggling to protect.

"I didn't know it had gotten so bad. I don't own a scale so I didn't know how much weight I'd lost. My clothes fit a little differently, loose, but I'd heard lots of people lose weight early on." She felt a burning pressure at the backs of her eyes and blinked to defend against the emotions trying to slip free.

She was supposed to be the one who took her responsibilities seriously and made the right decisions. She was supposed to be able to count on herself. Her child's life depended on it.

She swallowed and looked up at Jeff.

The man who was all laughter and easy good times hadn't shown up at her bedside. This Jeff was serious. No-nonsense. And he was here because the woman responsible for protecting his child hadn't even realized she was at risk of failing.

This Jeff had every reason for making an appearance. If the tables were turned, she'd be looking at him the same way.

"Jeff, I'm sorry."

He nodded, but the look in his eyes was hard. "Here's the deal, Darcy. I know you're tough and I know you're independent. But I'm uncomfortable with you alone like this. From what I understand, it was a fluke your boss happened to be walking by when you passed out. You work in isolation for hours at a stretch. Take public transportation home alone to the apartment you don't share with anyone else. You don't have anyone here looking out for you, so what I'm asking, is does it really make sense for you to still be up here?"

She looked down at her hands, at the plastic tube snaking its way up her arm, feeling more alone in that moment than she could ever remember feeling before.

"I've got a job here, Jeff."

He stepped closer to the bed, and after a pause, dropped into the chair beside her. His hand moved to her belly and rested there for a beat. "You've got *our baby* in here. And he's kicking your butt. Come back with me and I'll take care of you. We'll get through this together. You don't have to be on your own."

Darcy couldn't take her eyes off the sight of his hand against her stomach, couldn't think about anything but the heat radiating from his touch and how good it felt, when nothing had felt good, since the last time—the first time— he'd put his hands on her.

Which she couldn't think about. Not like this. Not with him touching her in a way that was so totally not about her at all, but about the child they shared together. About his concern.

Jeff cleared his throat. "We could get married."

Darcy stiffened. "We don't even know each other."

"I don't mean permanently. Just until the baby is born, so he'd be legitimate."

The breath leaked from her lungs, as she shook her head,

trying to ignore that pinch of disappointment there was no justification for. "Legitimacy isn't any reason to get married, Jeff."

"I know. Forget it." Jeff let out an impatient growl, pulled his hand away and then ran it through the mess of his hair going on as if he hadn't dropped that bomb. "You're determined to work?"

He couldn't understand, but he needed to accept it. "Yes."

"Fine." He stood, stared down at the spot where his hand had been and nodded.

Then heading for the door, he looked back with a frown. "I actually know of a position that might be the perfect fit."

CHAPTER EIGHT

"You low-down, dirty *liar*," Darcy accused, her color looking better than Jeff had seen it since Vegas.

Catching the finger she was jabbing into his chest with a gentle hand, he eased her back into the deep leather seat of the limo and clarified. "I never lied."

Omitted, evaded and manipulated? Yes.

Definitely.

But he'd taken one look at her lying in that hospital bed, and decided the moral hit was one he'd gladly take to ensure he got Darcy out of San Francisco and down to L.A. where he could make certain she was getting what she needed.

"False pretenses, Jeff," she hissed, her head working like a spindle as she shot nervous looks out one window after another as they rolled through the immaculately manicured upscale neighborhood of Beverly Hills.

"I told you, it was a part-time position as a personal assistant—"

"Oh, you told me all right," she snapped. "Flexible hours, excellent benefits including room and board, assisting an elderly widow with her social and charitable obligations—"

Her words cut off with a squeak as they turned into a private community where security waved them through.

"Hey, I never said *elderly*. I said *older*. Which is true." That's all he needed. The wrath of both his pregnant non-girlfriend combined with the wrath of his—

"Your *mother*, Jeff!"

The key here was to remain calm. Not to reach over and

haul Darcy into his lap and yell into her face about all the things *he* didn't like about their situation. About his lack of say. And her stubborn mule streak and the fact that she wasn't going to need a damn job for the rest of her damned life and why the hell wouldn't she just take one of the damn checks he kept trying to give her.

So instead, he blew out a controlled breath and met her enraged stare. Turned up his palms and shrugged. "She needed an assistant."

Okay, so his mother hadn't actually needed the assistant until Jeff called her and told her she did. But then, she'd rather desperately started needing one. Had been downright giddy about it, truth be told.

"Oh, does she? Your mother is so very busy, so lonely and desperate for help, she needs a woman she doesn't know moving into her home with her. A high school dropout, Jeff, who grew up in a beat-down trailer on the wrong side of the park. A Vegas cocktail waitress who went home with a virtual stranger, got knocked up and then—surprise!—showed up three months later. You think that's the woman your mother needs assisting her with her charitable endeavors?"

Jeff stared, wondering who was in this car with him. Because the woman he'd met in Vegas, the one who'd shown up at his office, and he'd been talking to every few nights for the past few weeks knew her own worth and would never in a million years let anyone undervalue her the way she'd just undervalued herself.

He understood pregnancy hadn't been a part of her plan, and he expected the loss of control for a woman who'd been all about the ironclad of it, had been a tough pill to swallow. He was certain it had shaken her confidence. But the words that had just come out of her mouth angered him.

"I don't know who to be offended for first, my mother, myself, my kid or you. Look, I don't come from a family of snobs. Yeah, we've got money and have had for a long time. But it doesn't mean we don't know the value of hard work, or respect people who've had to overcome challenges different than the ones we've faced. And here's something else. My mother respects me. That I took you home the night I met you will tell her something about you, too."

Darcy let out bitter laugh. "My measurements?"

"What the hell is wrong with you, Darcy? If it was just about your body—" And then he was right where he shouldn't be. Inches from Darcy's face, his eyes searching hers for any sign of the understanding he couldn't believe wasn't there. "Damn it, you *know* that wasn't how it was. *I wanted you!*"

As soon as the words left his mouth he cursed himself for saying them. Going forward as they intended would be easier without the acknowledgment of an attraction that was more than physical driving the hot pursuit he hadn't been able to shut down their first night together. But listening to Darcy sell herself short, he hadn't been able to stop himself.

Only now, as he saw the surprise in her eyes—the flash of hurt or remorse, maybe?—he realized she didn't know. Or at least hadn't been sure.

How could she have missed it? Why hadn't she believed him?

And what the hell difference did it make now? *None.*

Except perhaps to underscore yet another way in which he'd misperceived their initial connection. As much as he sometimes sensed that they were, he and Darcy weren't on the same page. He needed to remember that.

Jeff cleared his throat and sat back.

What mattered now was getting Darcy to agree to getting out of this car when they arrived, moving into his mother's house and if she was going to be bullheaded about the damn job thing, accepting the make-believe position of his mother's assistant.

Which meant getting her to settle down in the next thirty seconds before they reached the turnoff for his house.

"Couple things we need to get straight, Darcy. Here's what

I know. You've got your G.E.D., have a clean credit history, no criminal record, pay your own rent on time every time and until the past three months when you ran into some unexpected health issues, have had an exemplary work record. You don't fool around with customers...except that once, and you don't appear to do much dating. None of which is going to matter to my mother at all. The only thing she cares about is you are going to have her grandchild. That and someone else is going to be confirming the floral arrangements for her luncheon next week."

When she just stared at him, he stared right back. "You're the mother of my child. So yeah, I did a web search on you."

"All that came up?" she asked quietly, her brows inching up in a way that had the corners of his mouth twitching.

"No. It didn't. Now, stop putting yourself down. I don't like it."

The car pulled to a stop at the foot of the flared stone stairs leading to the front door.

Darcy shot a tentative look toward the house. "It's not like that's the way I see myself," she said quietly. "But I just don't know how someone who hasn't even met me yet could see anything else. And I don't want— If I'm living under the same roof—"

Jeff reached across the car and took her hand. "It won't be."

And the reason why, had just flung open the front door.

Darcy's heart began to thump, as Mrs. Norton, decked out in formfitting yoga gear and a disheveled ponytail, jogged down the stairs with a beaming smile and wide wave.

"Older?" she asked Jeff incredulously, wondering whether his father should have served time for taking a child bride. The woman couldn't be fifty.

Helping her out of the car, he answered, "She's older than we are."

"Jeffrey! Darling, it's so good to see you," Mrs. Norton

said, opening her arms wide to pull her six-foot-something son into her diminutive embrace. Then just as quickly as she'd pulled him in, she pushed him back, redirecting her focus on Darcy. Eyes that were the same warm hazel as Jeff's met hers as she held out a hand in welcome. "Darcy, thank God you've agreed to help me. This couldn't be more ideal. I was absolutely desperate and now we have the perfect opportunity to get to know each other. Ooh, I want to throw my arms around you, but Jeff would probably dive between us to protect you from my overzealous embrace. He's twitchy about you. If you haven't figured it out already."

Darcy shot a surprised look over at Jeff, standing there, hands hooked into his pockets, totally at ease in this bizarre situation.

"Mrs. Norton, thank you very much for opening up your home to me." She wanted to stress she wouldn't be staying long, but there was something in the open, welcoming smile on her face that made Darcy feel to do so would somehow be an insult.

"Oh, please, not Mrs. Norton. It's Gail. Believe me, five years from now when you're hearing Mrs. Norton every time one of this little guy's friends looks up at you, you'll know what I mean."

Darcy blanched at the reference to nuptials, but it was Jeff who jumped in to make the clarification. "Not *Mrs. Norton,* Mom. Ms. Penn."

Gail's cheeks went pink and her eyes squinched shut, but then she just laughed. "Oh, hell."

With a deep breath she waved her hand about dismissively. "I know. It's just the idea of having a little grandbaby— And as to Ms. Penn?" She shook her head conspiratorially. "In five years. Not a chance."

"Mom." This time Jeff's voice was more serious. "Don't—"

"Don't worry, darling I won't be pushing anyone in front of her until I've gotten to know her better. Why waste time with bad matches. Okay, come along now, kids. We'll get Darcy settled and then after a bit of rest, give her the tour."

"Honestly, Mrs. Nor—"

The arch look sailing over Jeff's mother's shoulder had her in place in a beat.

"*Gail.* You don't need to go to any trouble for me."

"Thank you, dear. But it's no trouble at all. Honestly, I couldn't be happier to have you here and just want you settled and comfortable as soon as possible."

"All right. Then thank you."

Gail nodded, her brisk steps taking her up the wide curving stairs to the still open front door. "I'm putting her in Connor's old room."

Darcy coughed, her eyes going wide as she looked over at Jeff. "Wow, *Connor* had a room to himself, huh."

Jeff was walking beside her, the strap of one bag slung across his chest. The handles from the other duffel hanging from his hand. "He spent a lot of time here when we had breaks from school." He answered distractedly, looking a bit tense all of the sudden. Was he having second thoughts about her being here? Or more likely he simply didn't remember the line he'd used to pick her up. The joke about his ego named Connor. But in truth, it was probably better there not be some collection of inside jokes between them.

The connection she felt to this man was dangerous enough without the added intimacy.

CHAPTER NINE

Up in Connor's old room, a space Jeff knew nearly as well as his own, he looked around wondering at what Darcy would make of it. The walls were still sage-green. The trim the same white that ran through the rest of the house. But somehow every bit of lingering high school boy and college man had been stripped from the space within the past day. The shelves emptied of all but a few items—and those last few he was certain remained just to ensure Darcy didn't walk into a space that felt barren and stark.

A gesture he appreciated after seeing how few belongings she actually owned.

He set the bags on the bed Darcy would be sleeping in. He'd never paid much attention before, but now, couldn't help but notice it was king-size. Huge for a single woman sleeping alone.

Which despite his mother's apparent desire to marry her off to someone—Darcy would be.

Mrs. Norton.

Not going to happen. Slip of the tongue or Freudian slip... His mother had been completely off base with that.

Darcy Norton.

He didn't know her middle name.

He blinked. What the hell was he thinking? He didn't need her middle name. Didn't want to know it.

Because even if there was some lingering bit of attraction between them, it wasn't the stuff *Mrs. Nortons* were made of.

Yeah, she was beautiful, and fun, and having his baby.

But Darcy was one giant no trespassing sign. And not in some sexual sense—but, damn, he needed his head to stop going there, too.

She was just so unavailable. Different than he'd believed that first night.

"It's bigger than my apartment."

He turned to where Darcy stood in the doorway, her arms wrapped across her belly signaling her stomach wasn't doing well, but hadn't reached critical levels yet.

"And it comes furnished, too. You'll have this room. The bathroom connects through there and you've got a sitting room with desk and computer on the other side."

"Okay, so it's a lot bigger than my apartment."

"Think you'll feel okay staying here?" It was such a strange question to ask, after he'd all but railroaded her into making the concession, swearing up and down she'd be comfortable.

Only now that she was precisely where he'd wanted to get her—the idea of actually leaving her here unsettled him in a way he couldn't reconcile.

Darcy looked around. Crossed to the window and peered out over a view of the pool and tennis court. "Your mom is kind of a firecracker."

"Yeah, she is. Make you uncomfortable?"

"No. It's nice. She's so…excited and welcoming. And it's a relief, but still sort of a surprise."

"Not what you were expecting." He knew, from those last moments in the car.

Darcy turned to him, a tentative smile on her lips. He could see how overwhelmed she was. And tired. And then before he could stop to think about whether it was a good idea or not, he'd crossed the room and pulled her into his arms. It didn't matter that they were strangers with this intimate past between them and uncertain future ahead. She was alone and he was there, and there wasn't anyone else on hand to give her the hug she needed.

For an instant she stiffened within his hold, and he thought she might pull away. But then she simply gave herself over to it. Bowing her head into his chest with her arms tucked up between them at either side, she let him hold her.

"It's going to be fine, Darcy. Give it a little time and all this is going to work out."

She nodded and took one deep breath after another, melting further into him with each pass of his hand over her back.

"I know," she whispered. "I'm just not used to being out of control."

Jeff let out a quiet laugh. "If it makes you feel any better, I'm not much of a fan of it myself."

"I've been taking care of myself since I was sixteen. I don't like...help. I don't like...needing things from other people. It makes me feel...*trapped*."

Her voice broke the smallest extent on that last word, twisting something deep in his chest.

Leaning back just far enough to catch the side of her face and bring it up so she was looking into his eyes, he promised, "Don't. Don't feel that way about this. About being here. About anything."

Their eyes were locked. Hers so vulnerable as she looked up at him, it made him ache to make it better. Made him ache to give her back all the things he'd seen in those eyes before. Steel, mirth, resolve, confidence...heat.

Hell.

Scratch that last. He didn't want to think about what she'd looked like when it was heat filling her eyes. Desire. Need.

Not when she was standing within the circle of his arms as he told her everything was going to be fine. When she needed reassurance. Not the muscle memory of some residual attraction she wouldn't be able to ignore springing to life between them.

But, she was so soft and warm and lush and...all the things he didn't want to notice. Shouldn't remember about the last time he felt her against his body, beneath his fingertips.

Setting her back a step, he walked to the door, not meet-ing her eyes as he spoke over his shoulder. "Why don't you take a few minutes and then meet us downstairs? Get that tour underway."

It wasn't as though Darcy had thought Jeff would be mov-ing in, too. She'd known he was simply dropping her off and then returning to the life he led in the city. They weren't together. They weren't a team. They weren't going to get through all this together.

They were two people, who were going to be sharing a child.

She understood it and had every intention of adhering to those mutually agreed upon limits.

It was just that in a day filled with so much uncertainty and upheaval, he'd made her feel safe. A little less alone.

And for a few minutes, she'd clung to that.

But now, Jeff was leaning in to kiss his mother's cheek. He'd already made certain Darcy had a list of two dozen phone numbers to use in case of emergency. And after a moment's hesitation when he didn't seem sure of whether to hug her or pat her arm, he leaned in and kissed her cheek, too. And then he left.

And Darcy stood staring at the closed door he'd walked out of, next to a woman she didn't know, in a house she didn't belong in.

Gail rested a hand at her elbow, offering a sympathetic look. "Are you all right with Jeffery gone?"

"I'll be fine. Honestly." It was so difficult to know what to say, circumstances being what they were. But meeting Gail's eyes she got the sense Jeff's mother was someone who ap-preciated the truth. "We hardly know each other."

Gail looked toward the door. "Give it time. You'll get to know each other, and figure out how exactly you fit into each other's lives."

The way the older woman said it, Darcy wondered if she

was holding out hope for a more traditional outcome for their relationship.

"Until then, you can take my totally unbiased opinion as gospel. Jeffrey is a wonderful man, who is going to make as wonderful a father as his was to him. And in case you haven't figured it out already, he'll do just about anything to make sure his child has a stable, happy home. You'll have everything you need. He'll see to it. And so will I. So…" She leaned in with a conspiratorial wink that was so very Jeff, Darcy almost did a double take. "Would it help even the playing field a bit if I started telling you stories about all the times Jeffery lost his lunch as a boy?"

"In what universe are we living that you, a guy who makes me look like a pauper, would move your pregnant non-girlfriend into your parents' spare room? You could buy the building next door to your office tomorrow. With cash. What the hell, man?"

Jeff gripped the wheel with fingers long gone white at the knuckles. "Give me a break, Connor. She's staying in your old room, so it's not like we're talking about some hole down in the basement with a moldy futon. She's got the entire west wing of the house to herself. She doesn't even have to use the same door."

"Glad to hear you aren't trying to smuggle her in and out through the basement window, but seriously, *your mom?*"

Connor chuckled from across the miles, his voice going muffled as he invariably filled in his new wife, Megan, on the details. Then he said, "Megan wants to know if your mom is making her pizza puffs on demand."

"Ha-ha. Megan's a laugh a minute."

"Man, I know it. She's great." Then quieter, as though there were a hand almost covering the phone, Connor said, "Come here, sweetheart… Great, see you in a few hours, gorgeous."

When Connor's attention was returned to the call, Jeff

let out a tight breath. "It was the first thing I thought of. She wasn't going to budge on the job thing. So I found her a job."

"Working for your mom? And Darcy's okay with it?"

"Not really. But for now, she's agreed. So it's a start."

"So what happens once she realizes Gail doesn't actually need any help with anything, from anyone—that if she wanted, she could probably add your job and mine to her mix of charitable foundations without breaking a sweat."

Jeff stared out the windshield, toward a sea of congested taillights. "I'm hoping Mom can keep her highly efficient tendencies under wraps for at least a couple of months. Long enough to give Darcy a chance to get some rest and me a chance to come up with my next game plan."

CHAPTER TEN

DARCY WOKE TO the unfamiliar and yet totally identifiable sound of lawn mowers from beyond her window. The sun shone in through the shades she'd neglected to close the night before, casting the room in a warm, golden glow she might have lingered in if not for her standing appointment with morning sickness.

Once taken care of, she showered, and then slipped into a pair of yoga pants and a thin, long sleeve T-shirt before heading downstairs. Gail had been gone when she woke up yesterday and only stopped in for a few minutes around late afternoon before disappearing through most of the evening, which had given Darcy the bulk of the day to familiarize herself with the house. She'd met the two housekeepers, Nancy and Viv, who had been incredibly warm and welcoming, right up to the minute she'd asked if she might help them out with anything. At which point those warm smiles had turned stern and she'd been pointed toward the couch and handed a glass of juice. Apparently, Jeff had spoken with them.

The break had been nice, but so much free time left her at loose ends, and she was looking forward to sitting down with Gail and finding out what her temporary position would entail and how quickly she could get her hands into something. Anything.

Stepping into the kitchen she found Gail standing at the farmhouse-style table a china cup in one hand, a tablet in the other. Stacks of folders spread out in front of her.

She looked up at Darcy's entrance and smiled her son's genuine smile. "Wonderful, you're up! Sleep okay?"

"I did, thank you. How about yourself?"

Gail nodded, quickly, then flapped her hand at the air as if to brush aside the morning pleasantries. "I'd like us to be friends, Darcy. Real friends."

"That would be nice," she answered.

"It would. So in the interest of friendship, I suggest we make a pact to be honest with each other. Truthful. Up-front. So we always know where we stand."

Nervous tension began to creep through her, because honesty had pretty much been the plan from the start. But maybe Gail wasn't as okay with having her here as she'd sounded when Jeff was around. "All right."

"Great! So I'll start. Now honestly, do you want to dive right into your made-up, fake job this morning or—" she clutched her hands in front of her, like she was making a plea "—go shopping for *baby clothes.*"

Six hours later, Darcy was on the phone with the caterer, confirming Tuesday's menu modification when Gail walked into the small office Darcy had made of her sitting room. Setting three binders on the edge of the small desk, she dropped into the chair on the opposite side. When Darcy wrapped up the call, Gail scanned the desk.

"For a fake job, we've actually scrounged up quite a bit to keep you busy."

Darcy let out a short laugh. There'd been a candid discussion between them earlier about the motivation behind this manufactured position. Gail had asked Darcy to put a pin in her frustration toward Jeff and consider the opportunity before her. If Darcy was serious about continuing to work—and she was—this was an opportunity to expand her skill set and open up avenues in the employment market that wouldn't have otherwise been available.

It was an offer Darcy realized she would be crazy not to

take. And within the hour she'd been on the job with Gail only huffing the smallest amount over the decision not to go baby clothes shopping.

Darcy reached for the top binder, only to have her fingers swatted away.

"*Part-time,* fake job. You agreed to take it easy for a few weeks, so this one will have to wait. For now, Jeff's got a friend of his—a doctor—stopping over in about an hour to check on you. Which leaves you some time for a phone call if you were planning to make one."

Jeff stared down at the phone in his hand, not sure what shocked him most. That his mother—his supposed number one fan and most staunch supporter—had completely, unequivocally thrown him under the bus in favor of his pregnant non-girlfriend. Or that Darcy had thanked him for what he'd done.

Definitely the latter.

And she'd sounded genuine. Excited even. Enough so the piece of her mind she'd given him about scheduling a doctor's appointment without consulting her first hardly stung at all. And in truth, he'd meant to call her about it, but then had ended up speaking to his mother and passing the message along, which had probably sounded more like a dictate, than the *on condition she didn't object,* he'd assumed would be implied.

She was going to stay with his mom.

She was going to take it easy with the work thing.

And for the first time since he'd found out she was pregnant, Jeff breathed an almost easy breath.

CHAPTER ELEVEN

"IF YOU DON'T give me that file," Darcy warned, leaning over her small desk toward the pilfering grandmother-in-the-making/woman-of-steel who happened to be Jeff's mother, "I'm—I'm—I'm not going baby clothes shopping with you this weekend."

Gail looked down at the manila folder she'd swiped from Darcy's hold and then looked back. "You said fifteen more minutes. That was over an hour ago."

She had. But after two weeks of taking it easy, Darcy's energy was back up. She'd regained a few pounds. And she'd found a satisfaction and meaning in the work she was doing she'd never had before. So on days like today, when the hormones ran rampant and her mood was a bit off, the work was her best distraction. And she didn't want to give it up. Besides, there was a benefit coming up to raise funds for a series of summer programs for at-risk youth. She wasn't ready to call it a day. Which meant she'd have to play hardball with Gail. "That little boutique we drove by Sunday... with the Frog Prince–themed window... I know you know the one. I *know* you want to go."

Gail got a sort of fevered look in her eyes. Baby clothes were this Superwoman's Kryptonite, and while Darcy mostly didn't like to exploit the weakness...she knew Gail would respect her for it in the end.

The file flopped back onto her desk.

"Fine. You win. But I was hoping to talk you into joining me for dinner with the girls tonight."

The invitation wasn't totally unexpected. Gail had offered to include her in her plans more than a handful of times over the past few weeks, but Darcy had yet to take her up on it. And when she made her excuse tonight, Gail didn't push but left with her usual, friendly "next time, then."

By the time Darcy found a good stopping place and turned off her desk lamp, the house was empty, the sky beyond the window glass already dark. Picking at a dinner her stomach wasn't interested in, she finished her book on pregnancy and motherhood. She watched five minutes worth of drivel on TV before turning it off in an impatient huff and setting out to walk the halls of the house, again.

When she reached the second floor, she turned toward her rooms but stopped instead at the first door on the left. Jeff's room. Normally she kept walking but tonight, she was at a loose end. As always, the door was open. And as always she experienced a tug of curiosity about the space within, and what it might tell her about the man who'd called it his.

Scanning the room, her eyes snared on the built-in shelves behind a desk. The rows of trophies and medals: baseball, tennis, swimming, football, track. The evidence of Jeff's achievements. It made her smile to think what he must have been like as a kid.

Gail had told her he'd been into mischief almost as much as he'd been out of it, but never in a way that was hurtful or destructive. She'd called him a rule bender. A perpetual charmer.

Traits apparently carried over into adulthood.

And if ever there was a man who made a bit of trouble look like fun, it was Jeff.

Pushing back from the doorframe she returned to her room. But her ping-ponging thoughts wouldn't still. Would she have a little boy or a girl? Was Jeff hoping for one over the other? What would labor feel like? Would Jeff be there? Would he stay cool? Hold her hand? Tell her not to be scared?

One question after another, and they kept circling back to Jeff.

How often would she see him? What would he do if they disagreed?

What kind of father would he be? She thought about the trophies and ribbons, and how nothing short of first place earned a spot on his wall of fame. Would he be as successful in parenting as he was in what appeared to be every other area of his life? Would he go it alone or hire in help? *Marry* in help?

Not the woman he'd been dating when she first came to him. Gail had mentioned they'd broken the relationship off already. But a man like Jeff—she closed her eyes trying to stop her train of thought, but already her mind had found the deep rumble of his laugh, the heavy cut of his jaw and the feel of his untamed hair between her fingers.

The weight of his body over hers.

The heat of his kiss.

Her eyes popped open. Because closed, well, obviously that wasn't helping. And as tempting as it was to recall their night together in exacting, vivid detail—it was a mistake. When she thought about Jeff now, it should be in the context of his role as co-parent to their child. Nothing else.

Which was fine. She was realistic enough to understand the enormity of the gulf between their worlds. She was okay with it.

Like she'd be okay when Jeff found the next woman to get serious about. Mostly. Though even as she thought it, some little piece of her rejected the idea of him with another woman. Not because she wanted him for herself.

No.

Just because…well…well…an irritated growl left her throat. It didn't matter why and she didn't need to justify anything.

What was wrong with her today?

Turning to happier thoughts, she tried to imagine Jeff's

youth, wondering whether he would describe himself the
same way his mother had? What he thought life would be
like for their child—if he'd want to do things the way his
parents had done with him, or if he'd like to see things happen differently for his own son or daughter.

She glanced at the phone and, experiencing a pull even
greater than the one outside Jeff's room, wondered if they
talked, if he'd make her laugh again, the way no one else
seemed capable of doing.

Jeff met Charlie's knowing eyes across the table where the
two of them had set up for the call in his office. It was time
for a break.

"Why don't we take thirty so everyone can grab a bite,"
Jeff suggested, pushing back from the table himself. "And
we'll pick up here when we get back."

Charlie went to grab a few files from his desk and Jeff
was left in the quiet of his office alone. Shoulder propped at
his favorite window, he was scrolling through his messages,
rereading the one line updates from his mom when the little
black-and-white, fifteen-week ultrasound image popped up
on his screen signaling a call from the very woman all his
extra hours at work were supposed to keep him from thinking about—but weren't.

"Hi, Jeff. I hope I'm not interrupting."

"Not at all. What's going on?" He closed his eyes. "Everything okay with the baby?"

His baby. *Their baby.*

The little troublemaker wreaking havoc on his mother's
system and scaring the living hell out Jeff with the fragility
of his existence alone.

"Oh, yes. Sorry, I should probably text before I call so
you know not to worry," she said, the words sounding almost amused. Playful.

He liked it, and found himself relaxing.

"What's up?"

"I was just wondering if maybe you had time to talk awhile."

He scanned the conference table. "I'm heading back into a call here in the next few minutes."

"Oh, of course, it definitely doesn't need to be now. You know, just sometime. I could come by your office. Or meet you after work—you're so busy, the evening would probably be better. But maybe not, because it's late and you're still working and I don't want to—you know what? It doesn't matter. It's not hugely important or anything—"

"Darcy," he cut her off, her fluster in trying not to inconvenience him somehow pushing a smile to his mouth. "Of course I'll make time. What is it you wanted to talk about?"

A sigh filtered through the line, and the sultry quality of it curled around his senses, rubbing soft against the places he'd been trying to ignore.

"I was just thinking this little guy is going to have a very different experience growing up than I did. And, I don't know," she continued softly. "I was hoping maybe you'd tell me more about what it was like for you. What you'd like it to be like for him."

Right. More information exchange, because that was the only reason she'd be calling. The only reason he wanted her to call. They'd agreed and for good reason. So yeah.

"How about this," he said, clearing his throat. "I'll get in touch tomorrow to set up a block of time when we can talk. Also if there's anything in particular you've got questions about or have on your mind, you can email me and I'll try to get a response back to you by the next morning. Okay?"

"Um. Sure. Sounds great, Jeff," she answered simply, but something had changed in her tone. There was no emotional inflection evident whatsoever. "Have a good night."

"You, too." He stared at the phone, suddenly on alert. Because he'd heard that total absence of *anything* in her voice before. In Vegas. When her impassive facade was hiding something she didn't want seen.

Charlie walked back into the office and within a few keystrokes had a modified timeline up on the big screen. He glanced at Jeff. "Want to go over this before we pick up?"

Yellow. Box mix. Cake.

The mouthwatering revelation had struck Darcy like a lightning bolt shortly after talking to Jeff.

There'd been a heaviness in her chest after their call because, inexplicably, she'd gotten it in her head that talking to him might snap her out of this strange funk. But she didn't feel any better. If anything she'd hung up feeling more adrift than she had before.

But what did she really expect. While Jeff definitely made her health and well-being a priority, the guy was busy. He had a life. Commitments to his corporation, his friends and whatever it was he did to fill his time when he wasn't checking in to make sure her blood pressure was where it should be.

So she'd hung up and sat at the side of her bed, wishing she could muster some enthusiasm for anything. Hating the way she'd lost her appetite completely and how nothing sounded good to her. It had been a full-on pity party the likes of which she never indulged. And then, in a flash, inspiration.

Cake.

Followed by something even more shocking still.

Hunger... Craving.

Next thing, she'd been rifling through the pantry, nearly bursting into tears at the discovery of one single cardboard box in the very back, and the tub of fudge frosting beside it.

Some forty minutes later she was staring down two eight-inch rounds, fresh from the oven, mentally calculating how long before they'd be cool enough to frost and eat. Too long.

"God," she half moaned, recognizing the near breathless desperation in her own voice. "I want you *so bad.*"

The sound of a throat clearing behind her had her jumping back, one hand moving instinctively toward her belly, the other going to her chest.

"Jeff," she gasped at seeing him in the doorway, tie askew, suit jacket flipped over one arm, shirt a perfect cut for his broad shoulders, looking rugged and powerful and thoroughly entertained with an amused smile tilting his lips. "I thought you had a call. What are you doing here?"

Rubbing a hand over the back of his neck, he nodded toward the counter. "Looking for some cake?"

CHAPTER TWELVE

SURROUNDED BY THE familiar dark wood cabinetry, heated stone floors and wide granite counters of the kitchen he'd spent a significant part of his youth hanging out in—it was with immense satisfaction that Jeff watched Darcy standing at the counter where she frosted the now-cooled cakes, her head tipped back as warm, full-bodied laugher bubbled past her lips.

"Traitor?" She teased, catching her breath. "She's *your* mother. And *you* were the one who finagled me into staying here and working with her. You had to know we'd find some middle ground."

"She sold out over a trip to some baby boutique? Come on."

He was crying foul, but seeing Darcy in person, his anxiety about her overdoing it was alleviated. Mostly anyway. And for all the noise he was making, he knew his mom wouldn't have skipped out for the night if she'd had even a moment's doubt about how Darcy was doing.

Darcy slid a fat slice of yellow cake layered with some kind of thick fudgy frosting onto a waiting plate.

Man, his mouth watered and he went to the counter, catching himself an instant before he leaned in to drop a kiss at her neck. Which was crazy, because it wasn't like this sort of domesticity was a habit. But seeing her there, laughing, chatting with him, looking so comfortable in her bare feet—it was like the scene flipped a switch in him and he'd forgotten exactly what they were doing and how it was between them.

Which was, not like *that*.

He slanted another look at her neck. Bare and long, and hell, with a tiny speck of cake batter along the side to match the few decorating her thin cotton hoodie.

She looked sweet. Tasty.

Because she was. He remembered running his tongue from her collarbone up behind her ear, and how the silky length of her hair had felt in his fingers as he gathered it out of his way.

"You okay?" Darcy asked, a wary look in her eyes.

Except for the way his entire body had gone online in the span of a few seconds, yeah, perfect. "Hungry. For cake."

Satisfied, she smiled and served him a slice. "Then here you go."

A *smaller* slice. Significantly.

"Really?" he asked with an arched brow.

Darcy flashed him a sassy grin and patted her flat stomach. "Eating for two. And since this is the only thing I've actually wanted in as long as I can remember." She looked down at her slice with a covetous intent and put on a growling brogue as she muttered, "Get in my belly."

Jeff blinked, not believing he'd just heard her quote an Austin Powers movie. He let out a hard laugh as she enthusiastically swept up her plate and went to the table, his little mama-in-the-making diving in without so much as a look his way.

Her lips closed around the fork and she gave up one of those unabashed moans that had his body reacting in a way where the best course of action seemed turning his back to her as he went to the fridge. "Think your belly's up for a glass of milk?"

Darcy was still sucking the frosting off her fork when he turned to look at her. Rather than just finish the bite, she continued to savor the cake and frosting, turning her fork upside down to suck the tines as she absently nodded at him.

He swallowed, gave himself a firm mental shake and then poured a couple of glasses.

They were drinking milk. And milk and hard-ons didn't go.

But even without the dairy, he shouldn't be thinking about Darcy like that. Because he wasn't ever going to *be with* Darcy that way again. Even if his head seemed to be making frequent sojourns to a time when he had, he had enough control to keep his body from following.

The pressure behind his fly told him he was lying to himself, but he threw a mental finger in that southern direction.

There was too much on the line with a child between them to risk emotions gone awry, which meant keeping it platonic.

He couldn't afford for things to end up the way they had with Margo. After all the years of friendship between them, in the end they could barely stand to be in the same room, let alone carry on a civilized conversation.

So resisting a few wayward urges shouldn't be too difficult considering it wasn't love they were fighting. Darcy was just so damned sexy, was all.

Yeah, their initial connection had been beyond the physical. But the part that *was* physical? He could still feel the embers from that blaze where they sizzled and burned in the back of his mind. Eventually though, he'd get past them.

Pulling it together, he slid into the chair across from hers. "So it's going well with my mom?"

Seeing Darcy was still working the damned fork, he shifted in his seat, adding tightly, "No rush to answer. Whenever you're finished molesting that fork with your tongue. By all means, take your time."

Her eyes widened, a satisfying rush of red tingeing her cheeks. It looked good on her.

Sliding the fork from between her lips in a way that didn't

do him any favors, she set the utensil at the side of her plate and neatly folded her arms in front of her.

"You mom is wonderful. I think she's one of the most generous people I've ever met."

Jeff smiled. "Did she try to buy you the house across the street—which incidentally is on the market if you like it. Smaller than this one but for the two of you—"

"No," she said waving him off with an annoyed glance. "She's very thoughtful. And observant. When I said generous, I meant with her time and her thoughts and feelings."

"She is, isn't she? I hoped she wouldn't overwhelm you. I know you like to be on your own."

Darcy shook her head, picking up the fork again and scraping at frosting left on her plate. Accumulating the smallest glob before bringing it to her mouth.

"We've struck a pretty good balance. We go for a walk each morning, sometimes just around the yard if my stomach is sketchy. We talk about interests and goals. And if ever I'm feeling embarrassed or something from having to rush away for my stomach, she always has some fantastic story about you to make me feel better."

Jeff's brow shot up, his ego taking a stretch and pulling him forward to hear more. "Yeah?"

"Yeah, like the time you got into the caterer's stash of dessert toppers and then got sick in the pool."

He slumped back. "No."

Not exactly the tales of heroism and maternal adoration he'd been banking on.

Darcy pointed the freshly cleaned tines at him. "Yeah. Her thinking is, it's only fair you share in the humiliation once in a while, too."

"I'm almost afraid to ask, but how often are you still getting sick."

There was a wicked glint in Darcy's eyes as she answered. "Often."

Jeff reached across the table and took her hand in his.

"Then I can say with the utmost sincerity, I hope you get past this soon."

She looked him up and down and then closed her eyes, laughing. "I'll bet you do."

She was so glad he'd come. Glad to the point where there was no choice but to acknowledge Jeff's little baby had been working her over good with the hormones.

Twice she'd felt the inexplicable push of tears at the back of her eyes. The first, when she realized halfway through her third slice of cake she was too full to eat any more, and the second when, at her request, Jeff had pulled his favorite trophy down and told her he had absolutely no idea why he favored it, and then after a shrug, stuck it back on the shelf.

Yes, the hormones were having their way with her for sure. Which was reassuring in that it gave her something to blame for other inexplicable reactions. Like every time she got within breathing distance of Jeff. All it took was the barest hint of his clean masculine scent and everything within her started to whir. He smelled better than box mix, but thankfully she'd exercised more restraint with the man than she had with the butter recipe.

As a result they'd been talking comfortably on the back terrace by the pool for more than an hour, Jeff answering whatever questions he could for her. Occasionally asking one himself—though in truth, Darcy didn't have very much to share about her own youth. If he asked whether she'd participated in some traditional all-American kind of activity, the answer was typically no. The explanation always the same. They hadn't had the money for team sports, camps or after school programs. Of course there had been more to it, but Jeff didn't need to know about those details. All that mattered was their child's life would be more like his than hers. This baby would be happy, loved and wanted.

They'd hit on the topic of school a few moments ago, and now Jeff leaned back in the terrace chair that looked more like it belonged in a showroom than outside by the pool. His long legs were extended out in front of him, his ankles crossed, hands folded behind his head as he stared up into the night sky.

"I don't know, Darcy. The boarding school thing was something both my parents agreed on. It's an experience I value. But with you barely halfway through the pregnancy, I don't really know whether it's something I'd want for him or her or not. To me this little guy's personality, drive and temperament will play pretty heavily into my position." His gaze locked with hers. "But whatever we decide, we'll decide together."

It had been the unofficial theme of their discussion for the night. That they were in this together. Not in a relationship way, but as far as working at keeping communication between them strong.

She nodded, letting him see the gratitude and appreciation in her eyes. "I believe you."

A breeze ruffled the leaves in the trees around the grounds and then caught a few loose strands of Darcy's hair, blowing them across her face. Tucking them behind her ear, she glanced up to find Jeff watching her with a look she couldn't read.

Suddenly self-conscious, she asked, "What?"

He waved her off.

"Nothing. It's late is all." He braced his hands on the armrests of his chair and pushed to stand. "You ought to get some rest and I've got to drive back."

Taking her hand, he helped her to her feet.

They walked back toward the house and, reaching the door, Jeff stopped. "I'll say good night here. Sleep in tomorrow, will you?"

At Darcy's rolled eyes, he flashed her one of those devastating grins that ought to require a special license the way he wielded it. "Come on, so I don't worry about you."

No question, this guy knew how to get what he wanted. "I'll do my best."

Satisfied, he leaned in—probably to drop a kiss on her cheek—only as he neared, the rich masculine scent that had been playing with her senses and control all night caught her off guard. Her eyes closed and her head turned toward him as she drew a deep breath through her nose.

Whoa—what the heck was she doing?

Her eyes popped wide, and there was Jeff, inches away, a darkening scowl underscoring his confusion.

Immediately, she took a step away to put more distance between them, but caught a heel on the edge of the walk.

Jeff's hand was there in an instant, guiding her back the way she'd come. Then closer. Until she was looking up into his face, their bodies only a breath away from contact.

This close there was no getting away from how good he smelled. Her heart was pounding, her breath coming too fast.

"Darcy?"

She shook her head. Trying to figure out exactly what to say when the truth—that she'd lost control and he'd, yes, just caught her going in for a whiff of him or whatever the cheap-feel equivalent would be for smelling someone up. This was so low.

"Honey?" His hold tightened as concern put an urgent edge to his voice. "Are you okay?"

She blinked. Okay? And then realization…she had an out here. Only her conscience pricked at the idea of passing off blame on her baby for her moment of weakness.

No, on second thought, she could definitely live with herself.

Raising a hand to her temple, she offered a weak shrug. "I think maybe I'm a little more worn out than I realized. A little light-headed is all."

The muscles of Jeff's throat worked up and down…and then before she realized what was happening, the man had her scooped into his arms.

"Jeff!" she squeaked, gripping his shirt as he shouldered his way in through the terrace door.

"I'll get you into bed and call Grant to come over."

"Jeff, no," she started and he stopped midstride to look down at her.

"Is it bad?" But before she could answer his attention seemed to have shifted inward and then he turned around, ready to carry her back out the door they'd just come through. "We'll go straight to the hospital."

Oh, hell.

"Jeff, no. Stop a second. Jeff. *Jeff.*" She squirmed in his arms, trying to get a leg down, but the man wasn't having any of it, at least until she grabbed his collar in her fist and gave it a solid shake, demanding, "Set me down this minute, damn it."

And then her feet were on the ground but he was still holding her far too close for comfort, especially because it had become painfully clear, she was going to have to own up to her crimes, or take a ride to the E.R.

"Darcy, if something's wrong—"

"Listen." She squared her shoulders, and dug up a bit of the no-nonsense steel she used to find so readily on hand. "I lied."

CHAPTER THIRTEEN

"You what?" Jeff's chin pulled back, his brows crashing down. "Are you telling me—all night? Has this been going on, all night, with the— Damn it, Darcy, this is serious. What the hell am I going to have to do to get you to take it easy, tie you to the bed?"

Her lips parted, but before the words she'd had ready mere seconds before could get out, her mind short-circuited and her eyes locked with his.

He raked a hand through the dark shock of his hair, and took a step back. "The chair."

Then he took another step back and swore under his breath. "I'm not going to tie you up at all. But—"

This *so* wasn't getting any better.

"Jeff. I lied about being worn-out and light-headed. I—I—" She took a deep breath and let the truth spill out in one huge gush. "You were standing so close—and this supersensitive smell thing that's part of the pregnancy, kind of got the better of me for one minute before I realized what I was doing, and then I tried to back up, but I tripped, and you asked if I was okay, and I thought it would be better to avoid any misunderstandings about me wanting to smell you if I just lied and blamed the baby, which sounds really terrible when I say it, but now that I'm thinking about it, is pretty much the truth. Your baby is making me crazy. There."

She sucked a great lungful of air and then covered her

cheeks with her hands, knowing they had to be burning crimson.

Jeff's jaw cocked to one side, his eyes focused down around his shoes. "So...you were...smelling me."

She crossed her arms and stared at the ceiling. "You smell...really good. It was like with the cake."

His head snapped up. "Like the cake? I mean, what you did to that cake."

And there were about a million wrong ways he could interpret what she'd just said, and based on the rapidly morphing expressions crossing his face, he was hitting on each one of them.

"I don't mean you smell like a cake. And I wasn't saying... you made me—"

Something dark flashed in his eyes as he looked down at her mouth. "Hungry?"

She nodded, thinking the way the night was playing out, they were going to need a couple of neck braces. "Right. No. I mean, no, you didn't make me hungry. I just don't want you to think—"

"I don't. And I'm not thinking about tying you to the bed, either." Then he ran a wide hand over his mouth, and the eyes that met hers were filled with some twisted combination of apology, amusement and heat.

She gasped.

"Okay, okay," he answered with a distinctly unapologetic laugh. "I *am* thinking about it a little. Now. But normally I don't." He closed his eyes and held up a hand. "Not the tying up part at least. Sometimes I think about the rest. I mean, we did it. And it was good. But it doesn't mean I'm interested in an act two. It's just a guy thing."

Okay. She'd take him at his word. "So we'll forget this then," she offered, not meeting his eyes as she thrust out her hand.

"Deal," he said with a firm shake before turning to go without a backward glance. "Now, lock the door and go to bed."

* * *

So the forgetting thing hadn't worked out. Which meant Jeff really should have stayed away from her. But that wasn't happening, either.

Rolling past security with a wave, Jeff pulled up the winding drive and parked around the side of the house.

Initially he'd thought he wanted the distance between them. He'd thought keeping Darcy at arm's length while knowing she was being looked after would be enough for him. More than enough.

But after the other night...hell. He'd been back three times in the two weeks since.

The first, because he wanted to make sure everything was still cool between them. The second, because everything *was* cool. And talking with Darcy was so damned easy. And the third...yeah, that's where his moral compass began to spin like maybe he'd landed himself in the Bermuda Triangle. The third time, like tonight he'd gone back to have Darcy to himself.

In a strictly platonic, or at least nonphysical way.

He might not be able to control his thoughts hopping the express train to Dirty Town when Darcy did certain things. Like laugh or eat cake or succumb to one of those mysterious blushes he figured it was better not to ask about. But physically, well, he'd kept his hands to himself.

With a child between them, they couldn't afford to risk souring their relationship because of some affair gone bad. Not when they needed to maintain positive relations...well, for as long as they both shall live. Forget the sanctity of marriage. They had to peaceably share a child. They were in it for the long haul. And really, if he looked past the whole out-of-wedlock, non-girlfriend part of the pregnancy, he was pretty damned lucky to have Darcy be the mother of his child. She made him laugh. Got what he was saying. Connected with him in a way that made him believe they could really make this thing—this parenting thing—work.

He liked her.

A lot.

Which was why he was driving out again tonight after spending the entire day and the majority of last night telling himself he wouldn't—reminding himself not to think about the way Darcy's hair sometimes spilled over one shoulder, leaving the bare length of her neck exposed on the other side. Or the soft curve of her mouth when she'd just finished laughing. Yeah, he'd figured some distance wouldn't be the worst thing. Tried to talk himself into a solid week before he saw her again. But after barely four days he'd gotten in his car and driven out anyway.

Throwing the car in Park, he checked his phone for whatever messages had come through between leaving his office and pulling in the drive, wanting them out of the way before he was with Darcy.

Not *with* with her. Though, sure enough, now that he'd made the mental jump—

He blew out a harsh breath.

It would be fine. So long as Darcy did her part to keep it wholesome…well, he'd be good for his.

Half a dozen hangers clattered together as they hit the bed, their high-end couture spilling across the duvet in a spectrum of linens, crisp cottons and stunning raw silks.

"Gail, please, I can't borrow your clothes."

The older woman turned a cool smile on her. "If you'd let me take you shopping like I wanted, you wouldn't need to. But now we're being picked up in less than an hour, and you need a dress for dinner."

Dinner with Grant Mitchel. The doctor Jeff had gone to school with and then bullied into checking on her a couple times a week.

When Gail had sprung the plans on her earlier that afternoon, Darcy had tried to put her off with the usual excuses. Only tonight Gail was having none of it. She'd looked her straight in the eye, smiling a sort of frightening smile and said, "You're going."

She'd seriously considered faking sick again to get out of it, because as nice a guy as Grant was, she knew the score. Gail was doing what she'd basically promised to do from the start— Trying to find her a nice husband. But after the way her last fib had blown up in her face she wasn't about to lie again.

"With you barely beginning to show and the loose cut of the pieces I've pulled out, all of these will fit. And if you want my opinion the burnt-orange would be fabulous on you."

Darcy opened her mouth to voice another protest—but Gail cut her off with a look that brooked no argument and a hanger against her chest.

Five minutes later, an airy sheath the color of a setting sun was skimming over her hips and belly in a silky caress. It was gorgeous, light and flattered her exactly the way Gail had promised it would. And more than anything she wanted to take it off, hand it back with whatever apology or excuse it would take to get out of a dinner the mere thought of was making her stomach roil with nerves.

From beyond the bathroom door, Darcy could hear the rise and fall of Gail's animated voice, but not exactly what was being said. A second, deeper voice sounded, and she stilled as her heart skipped a beat.

Jeff.

She swung the door wide.

"Why the hell *wouldn't* I join you?" Jeff demanded as his mother scoffed at him.

"Don't be dense, honey. If Grant wanted to catch up with you, he'd have set up some rock climbing retreat." She cocked her head. "He's the climber isn't he? Keeping all you boys straight can—"

"Yes, he's the climber. But you can't seriously be suggesting this is a date? Now? *He's her doctor* and she's preg—"

His words cut off when, pointing in Darcy's direction, Jeff caught sight of her, stopped talking and straightened, his eyes going dark as he stared at her.

"Hello, Jeff," she offered lamely, not quite knowing what to make of the interaction she'd walked into. Particularly as she was the subject…and yet not really a participant.

Jeff cleared his throat and wiped his expression clear.

"Beautiful, Darcy," he said, offering a polite smile that didn't reach his eyes. His hands went into his pockets, and she could swear she saw them ball into fists beneath. "Looking forward to tonight?"

There was any number of different ways she could answer. Most of them began with the word *no*. But out of respect for Gail and Grant as well, she was having difficulty voicing even one of them.

Gail began to collect the rest of the outfits she'd brought for Darcy to try. "Of course she is. Grant is a lovely man, and I know how appreciative *we all are* for the way he's given up so much of his time to *personally* check on her."

Ugh. The guilt trip. Even seeing it for what it was, her resistance crumbled. She had to go.

Schooling her features the way she'd done at the bar, she offered a nod.

Jeff stared at her a moment, a question forming in his eyes before his brows pushed high and he turned to his mother. "Oh, no way are you *making* her go out with him."

Darcy opened her mouth to defend Gail—but in a blink Jeff and Gail were going head-to-head.

"Making her? Please—"

"This is about that whole Mrs. Someone-suitable business—"

"She's a gorgeous, vivacious, available woman—"

"—can't even wait until after the baby—"

"—any man would be lucky to have—"

"I know that!"

"And you've made it clear you aren't—"

"*She's* not interested—at least not tonight. So she's not going. Period."

The truth was, she was too beat to care that they were arguing over her life like she wasn't there. Which really made Jeff's next move—pulling out his phone and calling Grant himself—probably for the best.

"Sorry, man, she's exhausted...no, I don't think a quick exam is necessary. Just some rest... Right. Mmm-hmm... No, you and Mom should go and have a great time.... *I insist.* I'll make sure Darcy gets whatever she needs." He shot her a wink and mouthed the words *cake* and *pizza* and something inside of her gave an almost painful twist.

Gail let out an infuriated growl and stalked out of the room, leaving Darcy and Jeff alone.

"I think I love you." She sighed, using the words in a careless joking way to underscore their throwaway quality, so there was no misunderstanding what had to be a look of utter adoration on her face. Hero worship for the man who'd just rescued her night.

Jeff flashed her his crooked smile, tucking the phone away.

"First a baby, now you love me." Nodding toward the door, he set his hand lightly at the small of her back in that gentlemanly way he had about him. "So if I'm reading this right, this is my window to propose?"

"I don't know, Jeff. What kind of pizza are we talking? And I want to hear more about this cake."

He leaned in close, so his voice was a low rumble just above her ear, so seductive she almost missed what he actually said. "I've got a yellow box mix in the car."

CHAPTER FOURTEEN

HIS MOTHER WASN'T speaking to him when Grant arrived. And, considering she'd been trying to set his pregnant non-girlfriend up with one of his oldest friends he could totally live with that.

It wasn't like he wanted Darcy for himself. He'd spent the past two months making sure everyone who crossed their paths understood he didn't. But did he want to see her set up with the guy who'd earned the nickname "Homer" in undergrad for all the "home runs" he scored on the female student body and a fair number of the faculty, as well. Sure Grant had grown up since then. Jeff had even set him up with a friend or two over the years.

But Darcy?

The mother of his child?

No.

The guy had been cool about it, too, shooting him a brief nod of understanding before ushering Jeff's mom out for the evening, and leaving Jeff and Darcy with the house to themselves.

He'd gotten her a pizza, and even made her the cake as they talked about movies and food, the work she'd been doing for his mother. They joked about Vegas and he told her about Connor and the wife he'd met and married all in one night, sharing a few of the more colorful highlights of their romantic journey.

Darcy laughed until she cried listening to his account of moving heaven and earth to keep a monumentally intoxicated Connor from taking the classic "drunk dial" to plane-hopping extremes in his quest to win Megan back after a particularly rough patch. And like always, the sound of her laughter got to him like nothing else. It did something to the space in the center of his chest he wasn't even aware of when he wasn't with her. Made him wonder if there was anything he wouldn't do to ensure he got to keep hearing it.

Darcy snuggled into the corner of the couch, her feet tucked up against the buttery leather as the last of her laughter subsided. "Honestly, Jeff, after all that I hope they name their firstborn after you."

"Firstborn, hmm?" He stretched back himself, feeling the tension ease from his muscles. "You do that more now, too? Find yourself making reference to babies when you never did before? My V.P. suggested making it a drinking game, everyone taking a shot of espresso each time I drop the *B* word."

And there was the little twitch at the corner of her mouth. The telling precursor to the smile she didn't try to keep from him any longer.

"I guess maybe I do." She met his eyes. "But it makes me happy to know I'm not the only one with baby brain."

"I told you. We're in it together."

"Glad to hear you're volunteering to share in the labor and delivery."

He ran a hand through his hair, watching Darcy as a comfortable silence fell over them. Labor and delivery. It was hard to think that far ahead when she was hardly showing.

That dress she'd had on earlier—hell, it had been so damn sexy. Hugging the curves of her breasts, sliding around her hips and thighs, and there for the first time, he'd seen the barest curve of her belly. He'd wanted to put his hand over the little swell, rub his face against the silky fabric and whisper to the child they were sharing between them.

The possessive impulse stabbing through him had been sharp and deep, and he'd nearly blown a gasket at the thought she looked like that for another man.

But then the craziest thing had happened. She'd given him one of her placid smiles, the kind so bland, it wasn't supposed to reveal a single thing about the thought process taking place behind it...and he'd seen exactly what she was thinking.

She didn't want to go. She'd wanted to stay with him, like he wanted to stay with her. Because they were becoming friends, and the lure of this mutual interest that went deeper than any he'd known before, was almost impossible to resist.

Darcy's eyes closed, her features falling into a gentle expression so soft and beautiful, Jeff couldn't look away, couldn't stop the words that came from his mouth next because he hadn't even realized he was thinking them.

"Why did you go?"

Those gray eyes blinked open at him, so unguarded he knew right then she hadn't understood what he was asking.

He had the chance to take it back. Pretend at asking something other than the question haunting him for five months already. But he wanted to know. Somehow, he needed to, despite the fact it wouldn't change anything.

"In Vegas. Why did you leave the way you did?"

Like he knew it would, the soft smile hovering over her lips evaporated into the air along with the ease and comfort that had been between them.

Darcy's arms crossed over the small swell of her belly. Defensive. Guarded.

"I had to go. I shouldn't have been there in the first place."

Damn it, he didn't get it. "Why not? We met. We had fun. We had chemistry. What was so horrible about one night of giving in to it? It wasn't like you made it a biweekly habit."

The look she gave him held shades of hurt he didn't understand. "I know for you, one night is no big deal. You meet someone, have some fun, decide you want to take it back to your room for the night...and you go for it. You're good with a few hours of giving in because you won't walk away bruised. You won't get caught up in feelings you don't want

to have. You won't start building fantasies about a reality that
has an expiration date of a couple hours from then. But it's
not like that for me. I've spent the past ten years being the
only person looking out for me. So I've been careful. About
my job. My time. My life. But then there you were, offering
me a night to do a few of the things I'd never done. Tempting me to break the rules and live up Vegas like it was my
last night to do it."

"And because it actually was your last night, you agreed."

"After all the years of saying no and doing the right thing,
I couldn't resist. I thought I had it all figured out. I was done
with work. I wasn't going to be around for any unwanted attention. You seemed safe enough—plus you seemed smart
enough not to dump me in a ditch after six hundred video
cameras captured us leaving the casino together."

The way her brain worked. He both loved and hated it.

"So I figured, what was the harm? It seemed safe. No
risk. Just a night of fun."

Her mouth pulled to the side and her eyes went to some
faraway place it made him feel good to think he might be
with her in.

"It *was* fun. It was great," he said, appreciative for what
she was sharing, but still not any closer to understanding
why she'd taken off without so much as a goodbye.

"When I fell into bed with you, I thought I could handle
it. We were both adults. You made me feel things I never
feel. And I wanted more of it."

The next breath she took was unsteady.

"I wanted more of your eyes on me, looking like you
couldn't look away." She peered back at him and lifted one
shoulder. "I know that wasn't really the way it was. What we
were doing was about a physical release. It was about sex.
And I was okay with it. It's just—I don't know, it had been
so long since I'd been intimate with someone—I wasn't prepared for how it would make me feel. And I knew the kinds
of things running through my head didn't belong there."

He shouldn't ask. But, hell, he wanted to know. "What things?"

Darcy turned to the window, hiding her eyes from his, but not the pink stain infusing her cheeks.

"That being in your arms made me feel like I never wanted to leave. It was something I could get used to too fast. Something I might hope for more of."

"Then why the hell did you leave?"

This time the laughter that passed her lips had a bitter sound to it. A sharp edge to warn him from getting too close.

"Because that's not what either of us had been looking for. You didn't pick me up looking for a new girlfriend or someone to settle down with. You picked me up looking for the kind of good time that happens in Vegas and stays in Vegas. A few hours of fun, remember? No broken hearts in the street. But the time we shared meant something to me, and I wasn't willing to risk tainting the memory of it with some awkward dismissal where you handed me my panties and thanked me for the great time."

"You didn't know it was going to go that way."

"I didn't. But that's the point, Jeff. I couldn't stand the idea of waiting around to find out. I didn't want to be the cocktail waitress tucked into your bed hoping you weren't going to kick her out before morning."

So she'd bolted. Taken the drastic, undoable action before he'd even had a chance to give her another alternative. It wasn't the same as what happened with Margo. Not even close to the betrayal he'd never seen coming. And yet that sense of somehow being cheated lingered in the back of his mind, prompting him to come back with the different ways it could have gone.

"You could have gotten dressed and waited for me to come back. You could have been the one to say goodbye."

"Except then I'd still have been standing there hoping." The vulnerability in her eyes was like a blow to the chest, momentarily knocking the wind from his lungs.

What kind of life had she had that a little hope was such a bad thing?

He caught her chin in the crook of his finger. "I wanted to see you again. I wanted—" He broke off and shook his head. "Before I realized our protection failed, I was going to tell you I wanted to see you again."

But then the moment he saw what had happened everything changed. If Darcy had been there when he'd come out of the bathroom, yes, he'd have been able to explain about the protection. They'd have exchanged information. He'd have promised to get in touch within a few weeks. But he wouldn't have asked her to stay. He wouldn't have tried to convince her to give him the next day or night or anything else. Because he'd have been too worried about the rest of his life.

Only now the worst-case scenario that had eaten at his gut for months was a reality and it didn't feel like the worst of anything. It was just...not what he'd expected. Yes, it had turned his life upside down. Disrupted plans for the both of them. But he wouldn't take it back. He was going to be a father. With months yet before he would be able to lay eyes on his child, the connection was already there.

"I know I shouldn't have left, Jeff. And I'm sorry. But I was out of my depth. And the truth is, even if everything had been different, if you'd asked me for more than a single night, I still wouldn't have been able to take you up on it. I was moving. That day."

"I have a helicopter, cars, money. I could have met you. Anywhere."

What was he doing, trying to convince her of the possibility of a scenario he knew wouldn't have come to fruition? Unless, what he wanted was for her to start believing in the potential of what might have been—because he wanted her to believe in what still could be.

Her head tipped back, and Jeff found his eyes drifting over the slender extended column of her neck, the soft spill

of blond down her back and the small smile playing across
her lips. Hell, was that what he was doing there? Had he
started to believe?

Darcy, closed her eyes. "Hmm. You would have buzzed over
to San Francisco for a night out on the Wharf with your
Vegas cocktail waitress?"

"Probably would have skipped the Wharf unless it was
where *the woman I met in Vegas* wanted to go." There was
no missing the emphasis on his clarification or the hard look
he gave her when he made it. But then the amusement was
back as he leaned in conspiratorially closer.

"I would have booked the first trip around business. Made
it look like I was playing it cool. Like meeting up just happened to work out."

What if? was a dangerous game to play. One Darcy had
made it a life habit to avoid. But as with so many things, all
Jeff had to do was flash a dimple and there she was, playing along. Flirting around a road not taken.

*If things had gone like this...which they didn't...it could
have been like that.*

And why not? It wouldn't lead anywhere.

"Just look that way?" she teased.

But then Jeff was looking into her eyes, the small concen-
trated furrow between his brows giving her pause, drawing
her attention to the way that *invisible thing* she could feel
but couldn't see shifted in the air between them.

To a slow spreading warmth skimming the surface of
her skin.

To one beat of time blending into another, until Jeff answered, "Yes."

With Jeff's eyes locked on hers and his make-believe
admission still hovering in the air between them, suddenly
giving in to this flirtation once removed seemed far from
harmless. Like it had become a dangerous thing with the
potential to destroy something important to her.

And Darcy wasn't going to let that happen.

So clearing her throat, she made a show of screwing up her face and pushing a wry note into her voice. "Hmm, sounds nice. But if you really want to know, I have an aversion to *Pretty Woman* fantasies." Then quickly added, "Not that I see myself as a prostitute."

Jeff laughed. "Geez, Darcy, what kind of childhood did you have? Cinderella ring a bell? Hardworking-maiden, working her fingers to the bone serving the wealthy-but-cruel stepsisters, sneaks off to meet a hot prince who doesn't want to let her go and then moves heaven and earth to find her."

The slender arch of her brow pushed high. "Truth?"

"Always."

Well he'd asked for it. "I've never seen Cinderella. Of course, I know the gist of the story. It's the one with the shoe where the prince sends some lackey out to do his dirty work because he can't be bothered and doesn't even remember the face of the woman he's decided he wants to spend his life with. I'm way more familiar with Julia Roberts being pulled out of her low income life by the wealthy, romantic Richard Gere. It was my mom's favorite. We had it on VHS and at the end, it was so worn the thing would barely play anymore."

For a moment she could feel the oppressive heat and stale air within the old trailer coating her skin. "I used to hate seeing my mother's rapt expression as she stared at the screen, that same infuriating combination of hope and hopelessness in her eyes.

"The thing is, Jeff, I was never really into the idea of some Charming sweeping in to rescue me from my life. My fantasy, from as far back as I can remember, has always been to take care of myself. To be dependent on no one." She sighed, giving him one of those lopsided little grins that did things to him he wasn't used to. "So much for fantasies, huh?"

"What's wrong with letting someone with the means and desire take care of you? I know your independence is important to you...but, Darcy, we made this baby together. You're giving it your body, your very lifeblood. At this stage the only thing I have to give is support to you in whatever form you need. Emotional. Financial."

Darcy looked at the man who had been nothing but generous with her from the start and wondered if she'd ever trust him enough to explain. If she could make herself vulnerable enough to share why she was the way she was. If coming from this life of love and privilege, he could even begin to comprehend what it had been like to feel hungry, trapped, afraid. Hopeless. To have such a keen awareness of how precarious the only existence you knew was. To watch the man between you and a fate too terrifying to contemplate, count out one bill after another with his grimy hands, wondering if, when he was done with the sick game he played, he would give up a bill to her mother to buy food, or if he'd make them wait another day. Or more.

She could still hear her mother's nervous pleading. *"Earl, don't make me beg."*

And the answering sneer, *"Why not? Why the hell should I give you anything? Or that brat of yours."*

Then those yellowed eyes searching her out across the cramped space, and her mother's sudden desperate agreement. The sight of her mother on her knees, laughing like it was all a game, but the humiliation and desperation evident in every forced breath.

"Hey," Jeff asked, his brows drawn together. "What's wrong?"

"Nothing," she answered quickly. "Nothing's wrong. I know how lucky I am in all this. And I'm very grateful for your support."

Jeff stared at her a moment more, but whatever he was thinking she couldn't quite tell. And then, "I don't want your gratitude, Darcy. I want you to feel secure."

CHAPTER FIFTEEN

WITHIN THE WALLS of his modern L.A. apartment, Jeff pinched the bridge of his nose with one hand and tried not to crush the phone at his ear with the other. Only Jim Huang wasn't doing anything more than delivering the news that the two weeks Jeff had just spent in Melbourne nailing down a new deal with Lexington Construction had been a success. The contracts were in hand and everything was a go. But after fourteen fifteen-hour days, a seventeen-hour international flight, customs, a trip home only to shower and change, then a four-hour meeting at the L.A. office, Jeff was shot. And this verbal confirmation of what he'd already ascertained through email was his limit.

"Jim, that's fantastic news. Get in touch if anything critical comes up. Otherwise, I'll talk to you guys Monday. Round of drinks on me tonight."

Disconnecting, he looked at the clean lines and open space of his apartment and let the silence settle over him. A half-eaten microwave dinner sat in front of him. The beer he'd cracked, down a single swallow. It was only seven, but for the number of hours he'd been running, it was definitely late enough to go to bed.

Only he kept thinking about Darcy.

He'd talked to her a handful of times while he'd been gone, and texted daily. But after having gotten in the habit of heading over to the house a couple of times a week, going this long without seeing her was making him itch.

He'd checked in with her earlier. Said he'd drive out tomorrow after he'd gotten some sleep and might make company worth having. But now...

Hell. He ought to just go to bed. In fact, forget the bed.

He flopped back on the couch and stretched completely out for the first time in he couldn't remember. Felt the ache and creak of a body running on fumes.

And didn't go to sleep.

Because he couldn't stop thinking about her.

His arm slung out from the couch, fumbling across the coffee table until he found his phone.

He'd just check in. And then he'd be able to sleep.

Punching in a few numbers, he waited for the line to pick up. "I need a car."

The house was mostly dark by the time Jeff arrived, the downstairs deserted, no sounds of activity filtering through from the floors above. Maybe he should have called ahead, but he hadn't wanted to risk Darcy telling him to stay put and get some sleep...because he hadn't wanted to explain he didn't think he'd be able to until he saw her. Only, yeah, looked like that's how it was going to have to go.

At least he'd see her first thing tomorrow.

On leaden legs he took the first flight of stairs, his brain zeroing in on the bed a few yards away. Except then he heard it. A noise from Darcy's end of the hall.

She was awake. Shaking off his fatigue he strode toward her room, his heart starting to pound at the sliver of light leaking out from beneath her door. Raising a hand to knock, he stopped short at the sound of a muffled sniff from within.

Then another, followed by some kind of low growl.

What the hell?

He rapped twice. "Darcy?"

A thud.

Then a squeaked, "Jeff?"

"Yeah, you okay?"

Some shuffling sounded and he waited for the door to

open. Then more shuffling, this time farther from the door. And finally she answered.

"I'm really tired tonight. How about we talk in the morning, okay?"

He stared at the door, his hand already on the knob. Because, no, it wasn't okay. He could hear in her voice something was wrong.

"I'm coming in," he said giving her a second's warning to cover up if she needed to before turning the knob and stepping into the room.

"Aww hell, Darce," he said, crossing to the little heap of a woman crumpled at the edge of her bed, like the hundred or so tissues littering the end table and spilling onto the floor. "What happened?"

"It's hormones," she sniffed, trying to pull herself together as she waved him off with one hand. "I'll be fine tomorrow. Go to bed. Please."

Right. Not happening. Instead he gathered her up against him, so her head rested at his chest and his arms closed around her.

"Talk to me, honey. Tell me what's going on."

For a moment he thought she wouldn't answer. But he waited her out, stroking a palm over that soft spill of blond down her back, giving in to the impulse to let his fingers play at the ends. And then it was as if the fight and resistance simply drained away as a ragged sob escaped her.

"I'm so tired," she admitted in a defeated, broken voice. "I'm t-tired of getting sick. I'm tired of f-feeling like every minute my body becomes a little less m-my own. I'm tired of being d-disgusting and weepy and wiped out and confused. I keep telling myself to hang in there, that things will turn around and I'm going to feel better, but I don't. I feel worse. I'm still sick. Instead of my body getting round, i-it's lumpy. And—and—I don't have *anything* to wear."

That last one she finished on a sob so tragic it was like a knife to Jeff's gut. "Wait, what? Anything to wear where?"

"Anywhere. Nothing fits me. Everything is—" she broke off with another wretched sob.

Okay, he was tired. Really tired. But something didn't compute.

"Honey, why didn't you get some new clothes?"

She had a credit card and an account his mother had finally gotten her to let him fund. There was *plenty* of money.

"These fit fine two days ago! And today I didn't feel well, and I didn't want to ask your mom because I figured I'd just go tomorrow.... Only now, everything I put on is all bunchy and rough and tight and scratching and—" the face she made was utter, tortured frustration "—*I can't stand* the feel of it touching my stomach. *Not. For. One. More. Second.*"

Her last words were punctuated by her hands fumbling around at the closures, jerking at the offending garments as she—holy hell—started stripping them off.

Jeff looked behind him at the door, then back at the woman in front of him who was huffing and puffing with outraged indignation over the way her clothes were touching her.

Hormones.

That's what she'd said.

He'd heard tales about the havoc they wreaked. The kind of lows they'd brought men to when trying to appease the women caught in their violent, unpredictable sway.

Hell one of his buddies' wives had actually called a divorce lawyer at his suggestion they stop for something healthier than fast food when she was in her eighth month of pregnancy. The guy had laughed when his wife told the story, but there'd been a haunted look in his eyes that said the fear never truly went away.

Which meant the decisions he made in the next critical moments could be the difference between his simply knowing to fear and respect the hormones and being left with that haunted look himself.

Darcy already had the skirt she'd been wearing unzipped and halfway down her hips, a blue streak he wouldn't have credited her with flying from her lips.

Tread carefully.

He backed to the door and, catching the handle, swung it shut and locked it without ever taking his eyes off Darcy.

Yeah. The gentlemanly thing to do might have been to look away. But instinct was telling him hormones were like the sea. Something he didn't want to turn his back on.

The skirt was balled up in her hands now, only to be thrown on the floor in spectacular tantrum fashion.

He shouldn't be registering anything beyond compassion, he knew. But that his being there wasn't incentive enough for her to shut it down, made him want to puff out his chest like he had something to crow about. Like after all the polite, and nice and thoughtful they had going on for the sake of the little life growing inside her...there was trust between them, too. Enough that she was willing to *let him see* what she was really feeling.

Which was enraged.

The buttons down the front of her blouse, which were definitely straining under each ragged breath, went next.

"I can't stand it!" She cried her temper boiling over to next level proportions.

And yeah, he was ready for her.

His hands went to his tie, loosening the knot with a couple tugs. Then the buttons and links at his wrists.

CHAPTER SIXTEEN

DARCY FUMBLED THE slim disk again and that was it. Her hands bunched into the fabric at either side of the row of delicate mother-of-pearl buttons she'd loved so much when she saw them in the store, ready to rip the damn shirt into rags before she'd tolerate one more prickly seam cutting into her chest and stomach.

Two big hands closed gently around her wrists, the warmth of them radiating down her arms as a soft "Shhh," penetrated the fog of her harried mind.

Her eyes blinked open and—

Jeff was standing in front of her, his tie undone, shirt open to his waist.

"Jeff." She swallowed past the humiliation-sized knot lodged in her throat and peered up at him. "This isn't what I—I don't even know what I was thinking."

Those earthy hazel eyes met hers as he shrugged first one shoulder and then the other from his suit shirt, dropping it behind him. He tugged the soft cotton of his undershirt free at his waist before pulling it overhead, and Darcy was left staring at the broad bare expanse of Jeff's hard-cut upper body.

And wow.

"You were thinking you were tired of being uncomfortable," he started. "That the morning sickness isn't something you can control but *this*—clothes rubbing too tight—is. After months of how you've been feeling, no one could blame you for having had enough. You've been pushed to the edge by circumstances beyond your control. You hit your limit and needed to blow off a bit of steam."

Her throat tightened as emotion different from the frustration, the bitterness, the humiliation began to work its way to the surface. Blinking back a fresh rush of tears, she nodded unable to voice the gratitude for his simple understanding in any other way.

The seconds ticked past and Jeff stood holding her gaze with his own. Letting her see the compassion in his eyes. The lack of judgment over actions that would have had most men backing away slowly—hands in the air, eyes on the ceiling, too uncomfortable with the messy fallout of emotions gone off the chain to do anything more than leave. But not Jeff.

He was giving her all the time she needed. Letting her know he'd seen what she was going through. And it wasn't running him off.

Drawing her balled hands from where they rested at her own chest, Jeff brushed his thumbs in circles over her clenched fists and the sensitive skin at her wrists. "Open up, honey. Let go and try to relax a minute."

His touch was light, a graze, and yet the barely there quality of it drew her focus completely. It felt good, those slow, soft circles a balm to her battered soul.

Her fingers unfurled, leaving her palms open to his touch.

To the same slow, soft circling attention pulling the tension from the farthest reaches of her body. Her toes and calves, the backs of her knees, deep in her belly and down the length of her spine.

Then he was resting her palms against his chest, pressing his hands over hers for a single beat before moving on, following the line of her arms up to her shoulders and then—

Her lips parted on a stunned breath at the feel of his knuckles brushing the sensitive skin between her breasts, at the cool air spilling over the deepening V of skin exposed as his long fingers deftly worked each delicate disk free from its catch.

She shouldn't be letting him do this, only she couldn't find the words to tell him to stop. She didn't want to.

His gaze skimmed slowly up her body and, meeting with hers, held as he helped her out of the shirt and gently set it aside.

It was so intimate. Standing there in nothing but a bra and panties, the only changes to her body since the last time Jeff had seen her bare were the ones he'd caused. Her breasts were swollen, her belly thickening in a soft and mushy way that wasn't yet round enough to be beautiful for what it was.

While Jeff was *everything* he'd been from the very first. His body displaying the kind of clean chiseled perfection his too-rugged face lacked. Tall and broad, tapered and taut, it made her want to step closer and take shelter against him. From the solitude. The cool night air. The exposure of her changed body.

From being alone for so very long.

Because this man could make her feel good. Like no one else ever had.

Her gaze drifted to where her hands rested against the banded terrain of his abdomen and then slowly, it drifted up, her fingers following.

"Here, let's get this on you," Jeff said in a tight voice, holding up the white T-shirt he'd stripped off to pull over her head. The cotton was soft, still carrying his body heat, and once it billowed around her thighs like a dress, he took a step back to remove himself from the intimate little bubble of insanity that surrounded her.

What was she thinking? While she'd been eating up the expanse of his body with her eyes, he'd been offering a public service by helping her out of her shirt. He hadn't even looked below her chin.

Because that's not what it had been about for him.

Jeff had been rescuing her. Talking her down from the ledge and resolving the most immediate problem at hand. A scratchy stitch in her shirt.

And resolve it he had, because nothing in all her years had ever felt better against her skin than the T-shirt she was currently draped in.

But, holy cow, she was pathetic.

"Thank you for this," she muttered, barely able to meet Jeff's eyes.

"Welcome," he answered, sweeping his discarded suit shirt up from the floor as he headed for the door. "See you in the morning, Darcy."

Jeff stalked to his room, every muscle in his body working against him, kicking and screaming, and trying to drag him back the way he'd come. To the lush warm woman wrapped up in his T-shirt looking like the kind of Sunday morning fantasy he desperately wanted to get back in his bed.

It wasn't supposed to be like that with her. She didn't want it. Hell, he didn't want it, either. Fine. He *wanted* it. But he knew there was a good reason he wasn't supposed to. And still, he'd unwrapped her like the present he'd been waiting for all year.

Yeah, his intentions may have been pure when he'd started. At least as pure as they ever got around Darcy. She was suffering and he hated it. After months of persistent nausea, the complete upset to her life, her loss of autonomy and every other consequence she bore the burden of—the guilt was eating him alive. Because all of it, everything she was going through, could be laid at his feet.

So he'd seen an opportunity to make something better— and he'd charged in like some nut job white-knight-wannabe with delusions of good intentions as he shucked his shirt and went to town on hers.

The only thing he had going for him was the fact that he hadn't looked once he got her peeled out of a blouse that had definitely been snug in all the right places. The fabric pulling against the swell of her breasts, and fitted to perfection across a belly only just beginning to soften in the most temptingly touchable way.

Not that he'd gotten more than the barest taste of it.

He'd been trying to help, not cop a feel.

Yeah, keep telling yourself that, chump.

Truth, the intentions had started out good. But when he'd rested her delicate hands against his chest—those pure intentions had hopped the express freight straight to hell. The feel of her fingers brushing his bare skin had flipped every switch he had and it was nothing short of divine intervention he'd been able to keep that sudden and intense *want* from shining like a beacon. But he'd shut down the visual tells. Ruthlessly. With extreme prejudice. Because this was the mother of his child. And aside from the fact that he couldn't afford to screw it up with her—she damn well deserved better from him.

Darcy stared out the long-vacated door to her room, a sinking, horrible feeling deep in the pit of her stomach as her actions flashed though her mind like a slideshow of shame.

She'd *stripped* in front of Jeff.

And then when he'd done the only thing he could think of to help her out—literally giving her the shirt off his back—she'd gone and eyed him like some freaking piece of man candy she couldn't wait to wrap her lips around.

She wanted to tell herself it couldn't get worse. But it was about to. Because there was no way they were going to be able to quietly ignore what just happened, chalk it up to hormones and sweep it under the rug to forget.

No way.

She had to apologize. And she had to make sure Jeff knew that brief disconnect with her sanity wasn't a regular or long sustained thing.

Hands clasped at her chest, she forced one foot in front of the other until she'd made it to Jeff's door—where she found him stretched out across his floor in a hard plank position, those powerful shoulders and arms working his body in one relentless cycle of up and down after another.

His eyes were closed. The muscles along his arms and back shifting and rolling, standing out in sharp relief as his skin incrementally darkened with each set.

"Don't do it," he muttered under his breath, dropping a savage expletive before shifting the position of his hands from flat against the wood to fists. "Don't even think about going back in there."

Back? To her room, or to something else?

"Jeff." Her voice was hoarse, little more than a nervous whisper but enough that he heard her. Because suddenly, he stopped. All motion arrested, as though someone had hit Pause on the remote to his life, freezing him in place halfway between up and down.

Then slowly he straightened his arms and turned his head to look at her. Starting at her feet and moving up the length of her bare legs and over the expanse of his T-shirt before dropping his head back between his shoulders.

"Go back to your room, Darcy."

He didn't even want to look at her. This was so bad.

"I want to apologize for what happened. I—"

"I accept." Jeff pushed slowly to his feet, still not meeting her eyes. "Darcy, I've been awake for somewhere around forty-eight hours, and as far as good judgment and restraint go, I'm about tapped out. The last of my reserves having gone toward walking out your door just a few minutes ago."

Forty-eight hours? She'd known he was traveling, had been thrilled at the prospect of seeing him again, but by the time he'd arrived she'd been too far gone to register much of anything beyond her intense discomfort and frustration, and then the overwhelming and incredible relief the man before her had provided. But now as she looked closer, the evidence of fatigue cutting deep lines around his eyes, the shadows beneath and the weary stance were unmistakable.

He dealt with her the best he could and then used the last

of his resources to drag himself out of her little circle of hell…only to have her follow him back to his room. Nice.

Only, something was off. If he was so exhausted…

"Why are you doing push-ups?"

"Damn it, Darcy, I don't think you get how close I am to losing it here." Letting out a harsh laugh, he shoved his big hands through his hair. "Do us both a favor and, before I do something we'll both regret, go."

"I won't regret it. Whatever you have to say, just say it. I can take it." They'd clear the air and tomorrow it would be a new day. "Jeff, please, would you look at me?"

A second passed and then another. Jeff's shoulders and chest rose and fell with one ragged breath after another. And then he looked at her—and everything stopped.

The eyes that met hers weren't the eyes of the amicable man Jeff had been these past two months. They weren't harmless. They weren't benign.

They were dark, intense and hungry. They were the eyes of a man who'd left restraint behind.

And then he was closing the distance between them, all signs of fatigue thrown off as he caught the back of her head in the cradle of one palm and her hip with the other. "Damn it, Darcy, I warned you."

CHAPTER SEVENTEEN

HE'D LIED. NOTHING could have warned Darcy or prepared her for the kiss Jeff delivered. Because this kiss was like no other. Like nothing she'd experienced before. Not even with him.

This kiss was a crushing, urgent demand. An almost angry claim. A brutal stamp against her mouth so searingly hot and unexpected it terminated all thought, all reason, all response beyond the most base, primal instinct within her.

To take more.

More of him. His kiss. The heat surging through her veins. The high charge current coursing over her skin in search of an outlet.

She needed it with a desperation she'd never known. And when her mouth fell open beneath his in welcoming surrender and his tongue drove between her parted lips it was as if the circuit closed and this hot, shared, sensual energy overtook them both.

Her fingers were in his hair, tight and pulling him closer into more demanding contact. Her body arching into a firm press of breasts, and belly, and thighs to meet the hard bow of his. Oh, God, it was good.

All that heat against her sensitive, so long neglected body.

All that contact and promise.

All that *want*.

She was drowning in it. Lost in the desire ratcheting higher with each thrust of Jeff's tongue. Begging him with every needy gasp and tug to take her deeper. Give her more. Make it last.

And it did, until the dizzying need for air had them breaking away, but only to move on in their greedy exploration. Hands roaming a restless path across her back and bottom, into her hair and over her arms, Jeff devoured her neck— each wicked pull of his mouth, firm stroke of his tongue and gentle scrape of his teeth acting as the trigger to another sensual detonation within her.

"It's got to be you, Darcy," he growled between deft flicks of his tongue into the shallow behind her ear, the palm of one hand finding her heavy breast. "If this needs to stop…"

He pulled back, his eyes burning down the length of her body before meeting hers. "I can't make myself do it."

She shook her head, hating the scant inches between them and the cool air threatening to carry *reason* back into the mix. "Don't stop. I don't want to stop. Just this once. Tonight. I don't want you to stop."

"Just this once." His thumb swept across the soft cotton at her breast, and again when it pebbled tight against the confines of her bra. "And then we put it behind us."

Nodding frantically, she asked, "Can you do that? Can we agree?"

"Right now I'd agree to anything." His eyes dropped to the straining bud of her nipple. Went darker as he gently pinched it through the layers of fabric making her breath catch and stutter at the pleasure piercing her core, the molten heat spilling through her center. "But yes, I can do that."

At the next decadent circle of this thumb, she moaned, pressing into his touch. "Jeff, please."

His eyes blinked closed in an expression that bordered on pained. "You don't know…Darcy, how many nights…I've replayed those two words in my head."

This time, Darcy was the one to still. The sharp ache in her heart, clearing the sensual fog surrounding her in one stab. He'd admitted to thinking about them being together in the past. But always in the context of some emotionally barren, throwaway comment, underscoring the lack of meaning behind it. But this time, tonight, there was nothing throwaway in his tone. Only they'd just agreed—

Before she could think too much about it though, his hands were on the hem of her borrowed T-shirt and he was stripping it from her with the same efficiency he'd pulled it off himself.

And then his eyes were on her, reverent, filled with an awe that made her feel beautiful rather than self-conscious about the way her shape had changed.

"You're so gorgeous," he said in a voice so gruff, she felt the deep vibration of it down to her bones.

Catching her behind the knees and back, he carried her to the bed and followed her down, their mouths fused in a decadent, promising kiss that had Darcy's hands coasting over the hard planes of Jeff's chest, working down his abs, and then fumbling with his belt.

At her frustrated whimper, he brushed her fingers aside and backed off the bed. His skin was flushed with a combination of exertion, restraint and arousal. His defined musculature flexed with every motion.

He ran his palm over his mouth and from beneath, she thought she heard the word *fantasy.*

But then he was back at his belt. Never in her life had she seen anything so sexy as when, inside of two tugs, he had the belt loose and his fly open. Her eyes followed the neat line of hair arrowing south of his waist and—

Oh, yes, please.

His fully engorged shaft was thick and dark and jutting out from his body at an angle that defied gravity. And though she'd seen him like this before—had intimate knowledge of how he fit within her—the sight of him was shocking.

Arousing. Incredibly, unbearably arousing.

Making every part of her achy and swollen. Needy. Desperate.

So she did the only thing she could think of, banking on it garnering the same powerful response it had the first time. Breathless and trembling, she whispered, "Jeff, please."

It worked, because before she could draw her next breath, he'd kicked off his pants and shorts, returned to the bed and, body half covering hers, was kissing her senseless.

Supported on one arm, he stroked her greedily with the other, running a possessive hot touch up and down her thigh, catching the back of her knee in one hand so he could pull it alongside his hip and make hard contact with the soft needful place she wanted him to be.

Only she was still in her bra and panties. Too many layers between them.

She was about to complain when Jeff rocked against her just right, and her breath caught and her mind blanked of anything beyond the pressing, immediate need for him to do it again.

Her hips tilted in wanton invitation. Her hands running from his shoulders down his spine as far as she could reach, her heels sliding up the backs of his hard thighs to just beneath his butt as the steely length of him rolled across the wet strip of thin cotton covering her sex.

"Yes!"

Dipping into the cups of her bra, he carefully worked the lace beneath her breasts and sat back, eyes locked on the erotic display he'd made of her.

"Darcy—"

But whatever he'd meant to say was lost when he lowered his head and flicked his tongue against the turgid peak.

The fleeting contact wasn't enough. Not when he blew a warm breath across the tip, either, and especially not when he brushed his lips in a wicked back and forth tease that on every other pass or so allowed the achingly tight bud to slide between.

More.

"Please, Jeff," she whimpered. "In your mouth. Please."

He groaned and closed over one nipple, drawing with a sweet suction as he slid a hand into her panties and cupped her tender flesh.

His touch.

She'd tried not to think about it after that first night, but there was something so incredible about the way he'd handled her. Like he knew exactly what to do, what would feel the best, how she liked to be stroked, when to tease and when to give her what she was desperate for. So in those weak moments when her thoughts strayed, they'd strayed to this.

His fingers pressing between her slick folds, playing over her cleft. One thick digit working slowly inside her swollen, slick channel, then a second, stretching and filling her in a way that was so good, it made her beg for more, open her legs wider and tip her hips into his touch.

"Yes," she gasped, head tossing against the pillow as pleasure rocketed through her center with each gentle thrust. The tremor of need built fast, gathering strength with each guttural bit of praise, encouragement and promise of more.

He drew her nipple into the wet heat of his mouth, suckling in a rhythm that matched the slow stroke of what then became three fingers.

"Oh, God! Jeff, please," she panted. "Please! I need. I—"

Her pleas cut off as his thumb settled firmly at the top of her sex and—

"Come for me, Darcy."

—her world came apart, sensation and tension from every extremity surging, together, crashing through her in wave after wave of pleasure that was sharp and sweet and hot and, as was so often the case with Jeff, like nothing she'd known before.

Holy. Hell.

Darcy was coming against his hand, the pleasure he wrung from her body more satisfying than if he was the one finding his release.

An hour ago, he'd been about ready to sell his soul to get some sleep, but now? He'd forgo sleep for the rest of his life if it meant more of the silky sound of Darcy moaning his name. Only the rest of his life wasn't an option. What he had was tonight, and he wanted to make it last. Draw it out as long as possible. Give her what she wanted first. Then start in on what she needed. And after that, what he needed to give her.

One night.

Hell, the dull edge of that thought was nearly enough to yank him out of this perfect moment. But with so few precious hours available, he wasn't going to waste them dwelling on the things he couldn't have.

When the last of her tremors subsided and her body melted back into the mattress beneath her, Jeff backed down the bed, peeling her panties off in the process. Then coming back up, he pressed a kiss against her sex, earning himself another pleasured gasp and Darcy's full attention.

Pushing to her elbows, she stared down the length of her body at him. And damn, he'd never seen anything like it before. The silk of her long blond hair hung in a sexy tumble around her face and past her shoulders. Her eyes were all bedroom, slumberous and sated while somehow asking for more. Her lips parted and kiss swollen in a way that had him fighting about a dozen depraved impulses at once. Her belly softly rounded. And her breasts—

God help him, he should have finished what he started in taking off her bra, but some primal part of him was seriously getting off on the tight, peaked bounty of ripe flesh, overflowing the lace constraint he'd only managed to pull partially out of his way.

Darcy seemed to have noticed where his attention had been snared, too, because she glanced down at herself and then arched a questioning brow at him.

"I look—"

"Like a goddess," he said, reaching for her and helping her to her knees.

He unhooked the back clasp of the bra that had served his purposes more than hers for the past minutes, and brushed the straps down her arms before ducking aside to retrieve a condom from the wallet he'd tossed on his nightstand. Then circling behind her, he pulled her against him so they were kneeling upright together and whispered in her ear, "Not of this world, you're so incomparably sexy."

The little noise she made suggested she didn't entirely believe him, but it was true.

She'd been gorgeous that first night in Vegas, but now he couldn't look at her without being blown away by the absolute lush perfection of her.

And tonight she was giving herself to him.

His erection was throbbing painfully with need where it rested between the press of their bodies. He had to get inside of her. Had to have what he'd been ruthlessly denying himself.

Pulling back he ripped open the condom—and Darcy turned, looking over her shoulder first at the condom and then at him.

Her eyes skated away and she quietly asked, "Do we need that?"

Which was when it dawned on him. She was pregnant. He couldn't get her any more so.

But that wasn't what she was asking.

Pressing his forehead against her shoulder, he told her the truth. "I haven't slept with anyone since we were together."

She stiffened. "Olivia?"

Her doubt made sense. Everyone had known it was serious with Olivia from the start. But in that moment, Jeff realized his need to make a connection might have been more a result of the one he hadn't been able to keep with the woman finally in his arms, than the woman he'd found to replace her.

"We didn't—we never had sex. I don't know why, but I just—" He'd found and manufactured one excuse after another for them not to, somehow managing to convince them both it wasn't about him. But it had been. Or more likely, about Darcy—whose breath had left her in a rush, though which emotion was behind that forceful push he didn't know.

"The condom, it's an ingrained habit. I wasn't even thinking about it, but whatever you're comfortable with. I can wear it."

She looked back at him again, meeting his eyes over her shoulder and looking almost shy. "I want to *feel you*. Inside of me. Only you."

His heart began to thump to a savage rhythm as some possessive part of him roared to life.

Only him.

He couldn't wait another second.

Adjusting his knees, he positioned his shaft between Darcy's legs. Groaning at the slick heat he found there, the skin on skin sensation that was only about to get better, he ran the length of himself through the spread of her folds.

"Lean forward, baby. I'll go slow."

God help him, the sight of her when she did was almost too much to bear.

Taking himself in hand, he notched the head at her opening, and at her eager plea for more, carefully fed the length of himself, inch by painstaking inch, into her tight, clenching sheath.

Heaven.

Bliss.

Nirvana.

Her bottom was pressed into his groin, the inner walls of her sex hugging him as he was as close to her as he'd ever been to another person. A part of him wanted to hold on to the connection forever, but another instinct-driven part urged him to move.

To draw back through all that snug, wet friction and then watch his uncovered length sink deep again, while Darcy's fractured, needy cries stroked all the places within him her body couldn't touch.

But he wanted more. Wanted to give her more.

Buried deep, he urged her upright. Thrusting slow and steady, he kneaded her breast with one hand, while letting the other ride the hills and valleys of her body to where she was slippery and wet for him. To the hot, swollen bud that made her inner walls clench like a fist every time he grazed it.

Made her mindless and wild and, for however briefly, *his*.

"Jeff, oh, yes, yes, like that," she panted, pushing back into his groin even as her knees widened in a plea for more of his fingers on that secret place.

He circled, the slick orbits closing ever tighter until at last, she gave him what he needed. Another throaty cry of release as she came around his thrusting shaft and against the stroke of his fingers.

And while she lost herself in pleasured delirium, the hand he'd had at her breast coasted lower until he was cradling the place that was theirs together, and he gave in to the fantasy that for those few moments, everything he wanted was within his hold.

CHAPTER EIGHTEEN

THAT WAS—
  She'd never—
  There weren't—
  How had he—?
  Wow.
  Darcy blinked, shook her head and contemplated a hard pinch on her arm, just to make sure she hadn't actually been dreaming. Only if she was, forget the pinch—with Jeff still dropping slow sensual kisses around her hips, thighs and belly—this was a dream she never wanted to wake from.
  Of course thinking like that was enough for her to give herself a hard mental shake and remind herself this was about one night. About the both of them burning off the last of a lingering attraction while it still wouldn't get in the way. While they had the chance.
  Only as she lay in this bed that was Jeff's, and yet not really, soaking in the attention of a man with a gift for spoiling her, she had to admit, at least to herself, her attraction wasn't going anywhere. So maybe tonight was more about the chance to act on something she wanted but knew better than to try and keep.
  And tonight what Jeff had given her was an experience incredible enough to keep her in fantasies through the months and most likely years to come.
  Eventually there would be someone else—another man in her life. Maybe. If Gail had anything to say about it, anyway. But it would have to be a very long time off. Long enough

for the memory of what being with Jeff was like to dull and fade. Because this, tonight—she already felt like he'd ruined her for all other men. And based on the glint in his eyes, he'd only just gotten started.

Crawling over her, he positioned himself between her legs, careful not to allow his weight to rest on her, but still somehow maintaining a contact between them in too many places to count. "Marry me."

Darcy blinked up at him, her heart freezing until she caught the playful mirth in Jeff's eyes and relaxed back into the bed. "Okay, but only for tonight. And only if you do that thing again."

Gathering her close, Jeff kissed her long and slow and sweet as if he too wanted to draw out the night between them.

"God, you feel so good," she whispered, awed by how true it was. "It's been so long since I didn't feel *bad,* I didn't even remember what this was like."

"It's only been five months, baby, and you've already forgotten? My ego demands I make a more lasting impression this time."

"Your ego again. Hasn't he gotten us into enough trouble already?" Her hand smoothed over his chest, her knees sliding up against the outsides of his solid thighs.

It was so intimate.

The eye contact. The touch. The press of his hard sex against the wet softness of hers.

They wouldn't have this again and she trusted him, so she told him what she'd meant.

"Besides, I'm not talking about the sex. What I'm feeling right now is more than that." Then realizing how he might take her words, she quickly amended, "Don't worry, I don't mean *love* or anything crazy. It's just…for once I'm not worrying, or sick, or uncomfortable or any of the other things. When I'm with you like this, I feel like everything is going to be okay. I feel…safe."

There weren't any questions. There wasn't any risk.

Braced on his powerful arms above her, he searched her eyes, a slight furrow forming between his own. "Then maybe you should stay in my arms."

Darcy stilled, not wanting to read...*anything* into his words.

He meant tonight. Right now. For a few more minutes.

His gaze darkened as he stroked her ear, down her neck and over her breast, where he circled her nipple with the tip of a single finger. "Maybe I shouldn't let you go—"

His words cut off at the quiet thud of the door closing downstairs.

And suddenly Darcy's heart was pounding for a different reason altogether than it had mere seconds before.

"Your mom!" she choked, trying to wiggle out from beneath Jeff, whose chin had pulled back and seemed to be eyeing her with equal parts amusement and irritation. Okay, and the lust was still there, too.

She shoved at his shoulders and he backed off the bed, muttering something about the joys of being a teenager again, and Darcy wondered just how many times he'd been caught in his parents' house.

Then getting back on track, she realized the only thing that mattered was that *this would not be one of them*.

Jeff already had his pants on, and tossed Darcy her bra and his borrowed T-shirt. Then ducked, coming back up with her panties.

"Relax, I'll head my mother off downstairs. Tell her not to bother you tonight."

Darcy coughed. "What? No! Jeff, you look like..."

He pulled his T-shirt on over his head, thankfully covering the skin she'd marked.

"...well, like you've been doing exactly what we've been doing in here. I didn't think it was possible, but even your hair makes you look guilty."

Jeff stopped and, one arm in his dress shirt, craned to catch his reflection in the mirror. "Geez, you're right."

Yanking the T-shirt on as fast as she could, she looked around. Though they'd never actually made it underneath the covers, the duvet was a crumpled heap and the pillows scattered clear across the room. One was even in the doorway to the bathroom.

"She doesn't still check on you before going to bed at night, does she?"

Jeff looked at her like she'd gone mad, and he thought it was adorable. Which was so *not* the response she was after right then.

"This is bad," she stated, dread settling deep in her belly.

"No, it's not."

"Your mother opened her home to me. And the second she walks out the door, I'm treating it like—"

Jeff was in her face, then cutting her off with a hard kiss before pulling away to meet her eyes. "I know for a fact she's left the house since you moved in."

"That's not the point and you know it. Button your shirt," she said, desperately.

"Yours is inside out," he returned, flashing a grin when she gasped.

"How can you be so blasé about this? It's your mother. In her house—"

"Technically, it's my house. But I know what you mean."

She blinked at him, then yanked her shirt off and quickly pulled it back on.

Jeff held up a hand, squinting. "Do you hear her? Because I don't. And for reasons I prefer not to get into, I'm pretty adept at sounding out my mother's tread on the steps."

Darcy arched an amused brow at him. "I can only imagine."

And then her betraying mind was doing just that and it must have showed because suddenly Jeff pulled her in close, tsking at her ear. "Mmm, naughty. I've mentioned how much I like that, right?"

Flustered she pushed back, trying to make her scowl stick.

"I don't hear her. So I'm going to make a break for it. Good night, Jeff."

He shook his head, catching her hand and threading their fingers together. "She must have gone up the south stairs. Stay."

Darcy looked down at where their hands were joined, felt the overwhelming pull of *yes* from the very deepest part of her.

She peered up at him, again seeing the fatigue he'd shaken off while they were together, but now seemed etched in every line and shadow on his face.

It made her want to wrap her arms around him, kiss away the tension and— No.

"Better to end it like this I think."

Because suddenly she didn't feel so very safe at all.

Watching Darcy walk out his door, Jeff was struck with the thought that at least this time he'd seen her go. It wasn't the blindside of Vegas, not even close.

Only witnessing the actual departure didn't feel a whole hell of a lot better than it had the first time.

Which was nuts considering the panic and urgency he'd faced that night, while tonight he'd agreed to the limitations up front. So what was his problem?

Maybe it was the fatigue which, admittedly, had reached critical levels. He wasn't thinking clearly was all. Once he'd caught a few hours of sleep, he'd have his head back on straight and his expectations as they applied to Darcy back in line.

CHAPTER NINETEEN

PERCHED AT THE edge of her kitchen chair, heat from the mug tucked against her chest warming the skin beneath, Darcy tried for a calming breath. Chances were good she wouldn't see Jeff today. The low rumble of an engine had pulled her from a restless sleep around three, and when she'd walked past his room on her way downstairs a half hour before, the bed was more or less made up, the room empty.

Just as well.

"Stay..."

With echoes of the night before still whispering through her head, some distance couldn't hurt. In fact, the idea of Jeff in the city, figuring he'd wait a few more days, or maybe a week before coming back did more to ease the tension within her than all the chamomile-infused air she been gulping for the past ten minutes.

"...Maybe you should stay in my arms..."

Who knew, maybe he'd need to go back to Australia and it would be weeks before he had an opportunity to see her again. Even better.

"...Maybe I shouldn't let you go—"

It would give her time to stop wondering about whatever had been hovering on his lips when they'd realized his mother had returned home and the thought was cut off. Whether he'd been about to say *tonight, at all* or *for a few more minutes.*

It would give her time to remember it didn't matter what

qualifier he'd been about to apply. The man couldn't be held to anything he said after two days without sleep.

"...I warned you..."

A shiver ran through her at the memory of the heat those words had caused and all that had happened after.

Yes, it would be good if Jeff got very, very busy and she didn't have to see him again for a long, long—

"Are you interested in dating any of the guys my mother's getting lined up for you?"

Darcy jumped at the gruff voice she'd mentally relocated to downtown L.A., sloshing tea over the lip of her mug. "Jeff! You scared the life out of me. I—I thought you'd left last night. Your room was empty.... Wait, what?"

Jeff stood in the doorway to the kitchen wearing a contemplative scowl and a sleeveless white runner's tank with navy shorts. His skin was sweaty and dark from exertion, his hair standing in a sexy mess of damp spikes.

"Because she's not going to let it drop." He stared at her, a dark look in his eyes. "Hell, you've met her. She's tenacious. And these guys aren't going to be the usual fare of tail-chasing chumps you've spent the past few years deflecting. If you decided you wanted one of them..."

Darcy pushed back from the table and went to get a dish towel to wipe up her spill.

How could he even ask after what happened last night? It hurt—but it shouldn't. She shouldn't give him so much power over her. Steeling herself, she kept it simple.

"No." And then because she couldn't stand the sight of the scowl he was wearing, she added lightly, "I shudder to think how *your ego* would take it."

His mouth kicked up, and Jeff walked into the room, going straight to the coffee machine. "Hmm, I like how susceptible you are to his plight. With that in mind, what do you think about packing your things and coming back with me?"

"What?" She most definitely couldn't have heard him right. Not with the way Jeff was standing there casually

brewing himself a mug of coffee while he basically blew everything they'd agreed upon last night straight to hell.

"Turns out I'm the jealous sort. As it applies to you, anyway."

Jealous. Where was this coming from? After her near-date with Grant?

"If my mom's parading Southern California's most eligible bachelors in front of you every now and then…" He shook his head, again running that wide palm over the scrub of his solid jaw. "Yeah, I'm losing it a little thinking about one of them catching your attention. Because you'll catch theirs. Every one, Darcy. So, self-serving bastard that I am, I'm going to be driving out here seven days a week with the straight-up intention of sabotaging her efforts."

"Jeff," she tried again, needing to inject some reason where suddenly there seemed to be none. "I'm a high school dropout. They aren't—"

"Going to care. Mom wouldn't let some stuck-up prick with a hard-on for credentials within ten thousand feet of you. But the men who would appreciate how easy it is to carry on a conversation with you about virtually anything— the ones who would respect that you've been steadily working your way through my old textbooks since you got here and read two newspapers a day. The ones who earn that laugh of yours—" Breaking off, he looked away muttering a coarse expletive.

"So yeah, even after I run the lot of these great guys off, the ego you keep indulging is still going to have something to prove. Which means…I'm going to be pulling out every dirty, low-down trick I can think of to seduce you back into my bed. And, Darcy?"

The dark look in Jeff's eyes did things to her she didn't want to think about. Didn't want to acknowledge.

Didn't want to stop. "What?"

He stepped behind her and, gathering her hair in a loose twist over one shoulder, ran his lips and then the stubble rough edge of his jaw along the sensitive exposed length of her neck in a way that made her breath catch and a needy ache stir low in her belly.

"I've got a lot of tricks. And I already know several that work on you."

"So what are you saying?" she asked, fighting the purr and moan trying to slip out with her words. "If I move in with you, you won't be compelled to seduce me?"

His hands slid down the length of her arms, then slowly back up as the low rumble of his laugh vibrated against her back. "No. I'll seduce you either way. But for a change, once I get you into my bed, I'd like to wake up to you still there the next morning."

A weight settled in her chest.

"Jeff, we talked about this. We agreed *last night.*"

"You can't hold me to anything I said last night. I hadn't slept in days. This morning, though, I'm seeing things clearly. I know you're worried about complicating a relationship we need to sustain for our child's sake. But it doesn't need to get complicated. What's between us—"

"Is sex," she stated evenly, though inside everything felt turbulent and chaotic.

"Yeah, really, really incredible sex. But there's friendship and caring and respect, too. And the truth is what I'm suggesting makes sense. You're pregnant with my child. I don't want you to be alone. And while you most definitely *could* stay out here with my mother…there's a very big part of me asking why you would, when we could be making the most of this time we've got before our little guy comes. We could take care of each other."

It was those last words that caught her, the balance suggested in *taking care of each other* that gave her pause.

"And what happens if one of us realizes they want more than the other? If one of us suddenly wants less? What happens if it gets messy?"

"It won't. We can keep it simple. You move in with me,

I make you feel good in ways that get you to give up those breathless little cries on a frequent basis, my ego gets regular feedings and we take all the guesswork out of it by putting a natural stop date on the fun and games when Junior comes— if we're open and honest about the limits of where this can go, no one gets hurt. We know what we're getting into."

He made it sound so easy, but it wouldn't be. Not for her. And yet what he was offering held an unmistakable appeal. It was the ready excuse to take more of this man she wanted so badly. The handy justification she needed to give in to the *want* without hating herself for being weak, for all but inviting the hurt and vulnerability some open-ended go at a relationship would involve.

If she agreed to what Jeff was suggesting, even if her emotions did get away from her, she wouldn't be waiting around for a happily ever after. She'd know there was a limit on the relationship and, having been a part of establishing those boundaries, wouldn't feel as though she'd betrayed herself by giving in. She'd have made the conscious, informed decision to grab hold of this pleasure for the time it was available.

And when it was over, she'd be able to look at herself in the mirror without seeing some pathetic victim with her hand out waiting for whatever emotional scraps were available and her breath held for some fantasy that would never come true.

She turned to face him, searching his eyes. "So you're talking about a sort of extended friends-with-benefits arrangement?"

Jeff winced as though he didn't like the sound of it, but then seemed to reconsider. "I suppose that would be accurate."

She wouldn't be his girlfriend. It wouldn't be a relationship.

It would be an affair with a bittersweet but predetermined end date. Something she could live with.

"What would we tell your mother?" she asked. "What would you tell everyone?"

Because people would talk. How could they not? She remembered some of the stories about Connor and Megan and knew the talk they'd had to contend with was nothing compared to the gossip and speculation that would surround her. Not that there wasn't plenty already, but if she moved in with Jeff...and then moved out.

"Nothing. It's no one's business but ours." His arms snaked around her back in an unmistakably possessive hold. "You're not going to regret this."

This close she couldn't think, at least not about anything beyond how good it felt to have him touch her. How much closer she wanted to get. Pressing her palms into his chest she pushed, trying to keep the action from turning into a shameless feel.

"Jeff, wait, I haven't decided yet."

The corner of his mouth kicked up. "Yes, you have."

And when he ducked his head to catch her mouth with his, there was no denying he was right.

For long moments he kissed her, slowly, deeply, thoroughly—the languid sweep of his tongue between her lips serving both to seal the deal as well as remind her they could take as much time as they liked.

And then from the hall beyond came the rattle of keys and Darcy jerked back, only to have Jeff catch her before she could put more than a few inches between them.

"Not done with you yet," he murmured at her ear as Gail's sing-songy chatter—a little more clipped than usual, spilled around the corner.

"Running late...Pilates...lots of errands...back later."

Jeff's brow arched and they both looked toward the doorway leading to the back door in time to see Gail buzz past with a hasty wave and barely a backward glance.

Darcy glanced up at Jeff. "She knows."

Jeff wagged his head. "Probably. On the upside, she won't be surprised when we tell her you're moving out."

CHAPTER TWENTY

THE UNIVERSE WAS conspiring against him. There wasn't any other explanation for why three times Jeff had gotten Darcy into his bed, and three times he'd woken up alone.

Rubbing the sleep from his eyes, he rolled onto his back and stretched across an expanse of sheets better suited to two than one.

He'd get up earlier tomorrow because he was determined to have Darcy in his bed, every way possible. He hadn't thought it could get any better than having her coming apart for him in this space that was his alone. But after the passion had been sated and they lay together with Darcy tucked into the shelter of his body—for once not going anywhere… the rhythm of her breath slowing until she was asleep in his arms, his hand resting over the small swell of her belly— yeah, that was a satisfaction, a rightness beyond expectation.

It made him want more.

Starting with the sleep-softened morning version of her lazing between his sheets. Warming beneath his unhurried touch. Giving up those little pleasured sounds he couldn't get enough of.

Pushing out of bed, Jeff groaned thinking how gorgeous she'd be in the morning with nothing but sunshine blanketing her lush body, making all that silky hair shine like spilled gold across his pillow.

Maybe he'd coax her back into bed, he thought, about to swing the bathroom door open—when Darcy beat him to it emerging from the other side, hair pulled back into a snarled knot, the skin beneath her eyes looking like an old bruise and her complexion in general making the slate-gray of his sheets look downright rosy.

"Darcy, are you okay?" he asked, wrapping an arm around her shoulders, ready to swing her into his arms and jog over to the E.R. She looked like death warmed over and suddenly a part of him was sincerely wishing Grant was the man she'd spent the night with so he could help her. But even as the thought skirted through his mind, a highly possessive part of him roared. Definitely no Grant.

"I will be," she half moaned then, looking down at her watch, added, "in about five minutes. It never lasts past eight-thirty these days."

Holy hell. This was the morning sickness she still endured a few times a week. Which meant it wasn't the universe conspiring against him after all. Just his little baby in the making.

"Do you want to get back into bed? I can bring you some crackers, ginger ale, tea, eggs or a cake—do you want more cake?"

She waved a frenzied hand in front of him, her lips pinching together as her cheeks puffed out, effectively conveying her "No thank you" in somewhat less polite but more effective nonverbal means.

Which left him standing there looking down at her with a sense of impotence he didn't dig at all.

"Darce, is there anything I can do for you?"

Shaking her head, she muttered, "Just give me a couple of minutes. Alone."

Alone.

Why did she always want to go it alone? And damn it, why did it bother him so much that she did?

Giving her hand a parting squeeze, he headed out to the kitchen figuring he'd make some tea for when she was ready.

She couldn't catch a break. Darcy flattened her hands on the solid marble counter and stared into the mirror in front of her. One morning. That's really all she'd wanted. Just the one to get accustomed to being with Jeff on an extended basis without her stomach rolling out the welcome mat for this new phase of their relationship. Temporary phase. For their non-relationship.

She let out a deep sigh. It was supposed to be *based on sex.* And morning sickness, hers in particular, was so totally not sexy. Not even close.

Her belly gave a twist of the more traditional dread-filled variety as she geared up to leave the sanctuary of Jeff's sleek master bath. If she was going to find regret in Jeff's eyes or discomfort or whatever else, she wanted to see it now.

She'd be able to handle it, too. Because there wasn't any part of her that had gotten attached to the idea of being here.

No, she was fine.

She was tough. Practical. And resilient.

A last glance in the mirror told her she was also about as put together as she was going to get. Freshly showered, teeth cleaned, hair blown out smooth and neat. Sure the blouse was a little tight and she didn't love the feel of it, but she was banking on the snug fit to give her an edge in the coming exchange.

Walking down the hall, her bare feet quiet over the blond hardwood, she took in the modern clean lines of the place— the open layout, high ceilings and stark-white walls—all contrasting with the repurposed hunks of heavy steel.

The apartment was so Jeff she couldn't help but love it on sight.

And she'd only just gotten there.

It didn't matter.

In the kitchen, Jeff was on the phone, issuing one word replies between brief pauses as he cracked some eggs, single-handed into a bowl with shredded cheese. He hadn't bothered to pull on a shirt and was still sporting those superthin drawstring plaid pajama bottoms with bare feet. His hair looked the same as always—messy in a tempting but touch-me-at-your-own-peril way. And the look was hot enough to nullify any advantage her too-tight blouse might have earned her.

This was the man who'd pleasured her senseless the night before. And then this morning—

Don't think about it.

Darcy slid onto a stool that looked like some kind of industrial spring with a leather padded seat top, and watched the play of muscles across his broad shoulders and down his arm as he used a fork to whip through the mix.

"Yep...Uh-huh...That's great...In about an hour, then... Excellent." Jeff thumbed off the phone and catching sight of her over his shoulder turned. "Hey, you feeling better?"

"Completely, thanks." That was the thing about the morning sickness, once it was gone, it was really gone. Well, until it came back. But the interim...she felt like a million bucks.

Darcy nodded toward the phone in his hand. "Do you have an appointment?"

"Oh, no. Well, yes. It's for you. Charlie got the name of a maternity boutique and coordinated the delivery of a selection of clothes this morning. No more itchy seams...you know...touching you."

Maternity clothes. Delivered. So she wouldn't have to go out in clothes that bothered her.

This man was thoughtful in ways most people would never think of.

"Thanks, Jeff." Then forcing herself to bring up what she really wanted to forget, she started, "About when you woke up..."

Jeff set the phone down on the counter behind him. "I knew you still got sick. But I haven't really seen the way it affects you for a while."

"Not exactly what you had in mind, I'm guessing." Not after all the seductive promises and racy talk.

A short breath. "Not exactly."

How could it be?

Jeff crossed to the counter where Darcy was seated and braced on his forearms. A muscle in his jaw started to jump.

Darcy forced herself not to shift on the stool, not to look away from his remorse-filled eyes when he said, "I'm sorry."

This was it. He was going to tell her it was a mistake. He shouldn't have asked her to come.

She'd agree, and look relieved while she said it, even if it killed her. Because she'd known better. And because what mattered was keeping their relationship amicable. For their baby and themselves.

"Don't be. Neither of us was thinking straight," she offered, backing up her words with a lightness she didn't feel. "Seriously, let's chalk it up to lack of sleep and pheromone overdose and—"

"Darcy, what the hell are you talking about?" Jeff demanded, whatever guilt there'd been in his eyes now replaced with a sharp accusation. Then, "Forget I asked. I've got it, but clearly you don't. I'm not sorry my morning sex kitten fantasy got rained out by a little reality. What I'm sorry about is you going through this alone. I'm sorry I haven't been there every morning and through whatever part of the rest of the day this sickness occupies from the start. I'm sorry you're so used to being on your own, that even now when I'm right here, you're more comfortable sending me away. Darcy, I'm just sorry it hasn't been easier for you."

"Jeff—"

"And you aren't moving out, so don't even start about it. I just got you here. And damn it, you're going to let me take care of you and you're going to like it." Catching the back of her neck with one hand and her stool with the other, Jeff planted a firm kiss on her, stepping between her legs as they softened together.

"You brushed right?" he asked, a mirthful smile quirking his lips until he looked down between them, apparently noticing the swell of her breasts within the too-tight blouse for the first time. "Never mind. I don't care."

He kissed her again. Deeper. Longer.

Darcy broke away, threading her hands between them to link around his neck. "I brushed," she murmured, leaning into the heat of his bare chest where she pressed her own soft openmouthed kiss at the center. "And flossed."

The next kiss landed at the tight bead of his masculine nipple, and was followed by a flick of her tongue and Jeff's rumbling groan.

"Baby, I love it when you talk oral hygiene to me."

Darcy couldn't help her laugh, even as her body turned hot and needy. Looking up at him from beneath her lashes, she purred, "I rinsed, Jeff. Mouthwash. A full sixty seconds."

His hands caught her hips, and without so much as a strained breath, he lifted her onto the counter, positioning himself between her legs, so they touched in all the most critical ways.

Jeff looked down into her eyes and let the humor fall away. "Darcy, let me be here for you."

And like that, the part of her she'd steeled against this man crumbled. Because when he looked into her eyes like he was, when he let her see how badly he needed her to let him in, there was no defense against it.

And so long as she remembered that no matter how good it felt to give in to Jeff, this was temporary…she'd be okay.

CHAPTER TWENTY-ONE

DARCY STARED INTO the half-fogged mirror, admiring the round swell of her belly as she turned from one side to the other. The swirling wisps of warm steam pinwheeled through the air as the bathroom door opened and then Jeff's reflection joined her an instant before his hands became solid, gathering the wet tendrils of her hair so it twisted to hang down her chest.

"Talk about an incentive to come home early," he murmured in her ear, their eyes locked in the reflection before them. Her, a naked bounty of soft and round and ripe, and him, a devastating contrast of disheveled and immaculate as always.

"Only in your world is seven early, Jeff."

His hands smoothed down the length of her back, his thumbs working gentle circles into the muscles strained from carrying the weight of two bodies in one. And then they slid forward over the hard swell of her belly, coasting in that reverent caress of here and there before succumbing to the temptation he could never resist. He cupped her breasts, gently taking their weight in his palms.

"Used to be your world, too."

"Yeah, but I wasn't at the office at six-thirty in the morning, either."

Those wicked thumbs made their first pass across her nipples and her breath rushed out in a shuddery gasp as she grabbed for the marble vanity in front of her.

She wanted to wrap her arms around his neck and bury

her face in the front of his shirt. Breathe in the masculine scent of him, but that would mean she couldn't watch.

Satisfaction gleamed in the eyes still holding hers as Jeff now brought his mouth to the curve of her neck, wetting that decadent spot with the slide of his tongue that had her body reacting in ways she couldn't control.

Her hips pushing back into the strong thighs braced behind her. Her lips parting on a ragged breath.

"God, I love coming home to this."

To this.

Not to her.

He loved this heightened, ever ready state of semi-arousal that had been the hormonal flip side to all those months of nausea. It wasn't news. And it wasn't a blow.

It was a reality she'd accepted and made peace with a month ago. Embraced. Because with his mouth moving against her skin, his thumbs making one slow circling pass over her nipples after another—she was so sensitive—his erection thickening long and hard against her bottom, she loved it, too.

She loved the release. Loved how sexy he made her feel. Loved the hot look he was giving her now.

And more than that, she loved the way this man never stopped surprising her. She loved the spontaneous unstoppable side of him that, last week, had him pulling her out of her seat at the tapas bar they frequented and spiriting her off for a night flight over L.A. in his helicopter. She loved that low growl rumbling against her neck every time he put his arms around her and the way, just before he fell asleep, he always pulled her that much closer.

She loved that he held her hand when they walked along the beach and, no matter where they found themselves, a gallery, the symphony or local market, the insatiable man always had something decadent and outrageously wicked to whisper in her ear.

And she loved that he knew it drove her wild.

It was so good. Like nothing she'd dreamed could be possible.

Not enough.

The words whispered through her mind, unwelcome, but not entirely unfamiliar.

Only she wasn't supposed to want more. She knew better.

But how was she going to give this up? How was she going to give him up when she'd already fallen—

"What's the matter?" Jeff asked, a furrow between his brows, his hands on her breasts still.

She shook her head. "Don't stop."

He stared at her through another beat, those too-perceptive eyes searching until she bit into her bottom lip, drawing his focus back to the need between them both. Then, "Please."

Their time was limited. She didn't want to waste a second.

The balmy night air surrounded them as Jeff watched Darcy suck and lick her last spoonful of brownie batter ice cream, if not totally immune to what she was doing to that spoon, at least in a place where he could control his physical reaction to the pleasured moans accompanying it. Though possibly his newfound control had more to do with knowing an hour before, he'd been the reason for Darcy's moans, and they'd put this paltry ice cream business to shame.

Still. He leaned close to Darcy's ear as they walked. "You know my ego's working itself into a snit right now."

Darcy slanted him a questioning look, her lips still wrapped around the spoon.

"With all that moaning, he's going to have something to prove in a serious way when we get home."

Her brows pulled together in some sort of faux apologetic look totally belied by the deliberate way she then slid the spoon in and out between her lips, adding a sultry little moan wholly different from the unconscious ones she'd been delivering moments before and Jeff's head shot around looking to see if anyone on the street was watching. But thankfully no one seemed aware, and then Darcy was just laughing, filling the street around them with that easy gorgeous sound he couldn't get enough of as she tossed her empty dish into a trash.

She was so relaxed now. Untroubled. Different from when they'd been making love and suddenly she wasn't in the same sensual place they'd been sharing the moment before. He'd let her put him off, but now he wanted to understand.

"Earlier tonight, Darcy, where did you go?"

She knew what he was talking about. He could see it in the instant of deliberation flashing through her eyes before she made the decision to trust him with the truth.

"I never realized what I was missing before," she answered, staring down the street ahead of them. "I mean I saw couples together, saw them having fun, but I always wondered what happened when they went home and no one was around to see, whether those bright smiles turned to fear."

Jeff's stomach turned to lead, and he pulled Darcy to a stop. "Did someone make you afraid?"

She seemed to consider, almost as if she didn't know the answer. In the end, though, she found her way to it. "Not a boyfriend of my own. I didn't really let guys get that close. But yes. My mom wasn't so discriminating and some of the guys who took us in—they made me scared."

He couldn't breathe. Couldn't do anything but take her hand because he needed to hold it, and wait for her to tell him the rest.

"Some of them had tempers that could get physical. And some of them would look at me in ways they shouldn't. And some of them just liked to play the kind of control games that might mean going hungry or not being able to go to school or to sleep."

"How the hell could she have let you live like that?" he asked, sickened and enraged by the actions of a woman he knew to have died in a car accident years before.

Darcy wouldn't meet his eyes. And when she answered, the hollow sound of her voice was like a blade to his heart.

"She said she didn't have a choice and we'd starve without someone to take care of us. She told me she couldn't risk leaving me alone with them to get a job, that we couldn't leave until she found someone else. Someone better. But that was a joke. The guys she found..." She shook her head. "I don't know what was wrong with her. But the guys she gravitated to were all just different shades of the same sick. And the worst of it was, I actually believed she didn't have a choice. I thought she was trapped the same way I was. I didn't know there were programs to help us. I didn't know she was actually choosing to live that way, to make me live that way until I got the full-time job that let me pay rent. Now that I'm going to be a mother and the need to protect this baby is so strong within me, it's like a tangible thing—more than ever I want to know why. But it's too late to ask, and I don't think I could have believed anything she said anyway."

Jeff pulled her into his arms, stroking her hair as a part of him died inside thinking of those beautiful gray eyes he'd seen so many ways filled with fear, their innocence draining away years too soon.

"Baby, I'm so sorry."

Now he got it. This was why she'd dropped out of school.

Why she'd been afraid to trust him enough to let him take care of her.

Why with all the money and resources at his disposal, he'd never be able to give her the thing she wanted most in her life. To be totally independent. And worse, that hard-won freedom she'd sacrificed so much for? He was the reason she'd lost it. He'd taken it away.

And when he looked at the round swell of her belly, he couldn't even regret it.

All he could do was show her there was another way. Prove that he never wanted to hold her back or hem her in or take away the opportunities available to her. He'd make certain she never felt trapped because of him again. She'd never need to escape.

Cradling her jaw in his hands he met her eyes.

"I know you don't believe in the fairy-tale rescues and you've already saved yourself, Darcy, but I'm behind you now, too. Nothing will ever be like that again. Not for you. Not for our baby. I swear it."

Blinking back tears, Darcy nodded and said the most amazing thing. "I already know."

"Locker-room talk?" Connor scoffed, his voice oozing the kind of censure only a best friend could muster. "I thought you were above all that."

Jeff paused in the act of relocating the stacks of papers and files from his desk to a mirror position on the conference table at the other end of the office.

"It's not like I'm starting a daily blog." He looked at the half-cleared desk, and then at the clock, his heart kicking up. "But *holy hell,* man—"

"Yeah, I've got it. The hormones. They're like the sea. And the tide's turned or whatever."

"She was at the door. Waiting, Connor. *At the door.* I didn't make it past the coat stand. *For. An. Hour.*"

Connor made an indifferent noise that had Jeff shaking his head in stunned disbelief.

"Good to hear she's feeling better. So what's Gail think about the move?"

"Yeah, yeah, Darcy's feeling much better. Aside from the mornings, she hasn't been sick for about two weeks. And my mom—she's not pressing. I told her I was more comfortable with Darcy staying with me. Didn't want to miss out on anything, yada, yada, yada. But forget about my mom and pay attention. About the hormones, because seriously, you and Megan might want to—"

"Enough. I get it. The sex with your pregnant non-girlfriend lover—"

"Darcy."

"Okay, sex with Darcy is insane. But I'm starting to feel a shade dirty, hearing about it."

Jeff stalled where he was. Yeah, truth was, he didn't want Connor thinking about Darcy like that, either. He wasn't nuts about the few details he'd been subjected to about Megan. There was just something different about being subjected to details about a guy's wife.

Not that Darcy was his wife.

The intercom from his desk sounded. "Ms. Penn here to see you."

With a quick goodbye for Connor, Jeff started to return the phone to his pants pocket, then thinking better of it, tossed it onto a chair. In one sweep, he had the rest of his desk cleared and the stack dumped in a heap on the conference table. And then he was striding to the door, swinging it open with a welcome greeting that didn't make it past his lips once he saw Darcy waiting for him in a shirt he knew for a fact she'd decided was too tight the week before. His eyes went momentarily unfocused as his tongue all but rolled out of his mouth.

"Hi, Jeff," she said. And he was sure it sounded completely innocuous to anyone who hadn't heard all the incredibly, fantastically naughty things coming out of her mouth when she'd called him thirty minutes before.

"Darcy, glad you could come. By. To talk." He coughed into his hand, mentally giving himself a violent shake. "Come on in."

Her gauzy layered skirt swung around her calves, showing off the slender turn of her ankles and hinting at the sexy length of what hid beneath.

Pulling his door closed behind them, he ducked back out offering a quick, "Hold my calls."

And then Darcy had hold of his tie and was pulling him deeper into his office. Tugging at him with hands that were everywhere at once.

"I don't know what's wrong with me," she gasped, when he jerked his tie loose and was halfway down the buttons of his shirt. "Faster."

"Wrong with you? Not one damn thing," he assured, wishing he had four hands instead of two so he could get them both naked in the next six point two seconds. Because now that she was here, he needed to make good on the promise she'd breathlessly reminded him of from the backseat of her car.

"You said you'd take care of me."

Apparently she'd been at the organic market shopping for dinner when she'd started feeling *restless* as she'd explained it. And then she'd started thinking about his desk. The high shine airplane wing that was the prize in his collection. With him *on it.*

Jeff freed the last button and started in on his fly, at which point he realized Darcy's eyes had glazed with lust and she'd only gotten her blouse half open before abandoning the task, in lieu of watching him strip.

Which reminded him of the night at his mother's house...

Slowing it down, Jeff methodically unbuckled his belt and then pulled it free of the loops.

"What—what are you doing?" Darcy asked, the breathless tremble in her words sending blood pounding toward his groin.

"Making you wait." He rolled the belt and set it on the desk chair. And shrugged one shoulder out of his shirt and then the other. "Letting you watch."

Darcy blinked in rapid repetition, her throat making some effort at words that didn't get past a few clicks.

Crossing his arms to reach for opposite sides of his T-shirt, he eased it up, getting hotter and harder with every grueling second that passed of watching Darcy watch him. Yeah, slow was definitely better than fast. This time.

He pulled the T-shirt overhead and Darcy let out a little sigh, spurring him on. His hands went to his pants, to the top button, the tab of his zipper, then lower as it traveled down, the teeth straining against his hard-on. He leaned back against his desk, shirtless, his pants open, his erection beyond the point of containment as it pushed past the top of his boxer briefs.

"Your body," she murmured, those smoky, soft gray eyes flitting to his for a moment of contact. "Is my very favorite plaything."

Shoving the briefs beneath his sac, he took himself in hand. "And you said we had nothing in common."

Darcy sucked a harsh breath, as he firmed his grip and rode up and down the length of his shaft with a few slow, sure strokes.

"Oh, God," she whimpered, wetting her lips with the sexy pink tip of her tongue. "I—I— You— I'm so—"

"Yeah," he groaned, "me, too. Take off your blouse for me, gorgeous."

Without taking her eyes off the up and down cycle of his hand, she undid her shirt, slipping out of it and letting it flutter to the ground, as her hands found the soft, ripe mounds of breasts that seemed to be growing in proportion to her belly.

"Like this?" she asked, the flush of excitement pinkening her skin as she ran her shaking open palms against the stiff points of her nipples.

"Yes." Immediately he eased up on his grip, because, holy hell, add Darcy touching herself while she watched him? A man knew his limits. "Your skirt, too."

Catching her bottom lip in the clasp of her teeth she gingerly stepped over to his desk chair and sat down. He stalled, wondering what—but then she was inching the filmy layers of her skirt up one teasing inch at a time, until he could see what she was most deliberately showing him.

And the world ceased to spin.

"Panties?" he choked out.

"Didn't think I was going to need them," she said with

that mind-blowing mix of shy minx as she reached between her legs.

He couldn't be seeing what he thought he was seeing. Even if he'd started this game and she seemed to like it a lot, she'd been shy about it. So this couldn't—

"Letting you watch," she moaned, reading the question in his eyes. "Making you wait."

One slender brow arched his way and suddenly, his gorgeous girl was in the power position. And he was all for letting her have it. For the next few minutes anyway.

"Don't stop, Jeff."

He resumed his stroke, fighting for control as he watched Darcy's fingers play at the place he desperately wanted to visit. She was slick and swollen, panting and ready, and getting close to the peak he wanted to take her to himself.

Needed to take her to himself.

This game had gone on long enough.

Going to his knees, he caught Darcy by the backs of hers and wheeled the chair closer.

A moment more and their discarded shirts were tucked behind her back, her hips were at the edge of the chair and her legs trembled atop his shoulders as he licked and kissed and teased her.

And then slowly, so slowly, so she wouldn't miss a second of what was happening, and he wouldn't miss a second of her response, he made a firm point of his tongue and sank into her waiting center.

"Jeff!"

His name hit with the first clench of her sex because all it had taken was one slow thrust and she'd come apart around his tongue. And because he wasn't ready to give up even one second he could have of this, he continued to lap and kiss and stroke her until he'd coaxed the very last shudder from her body.

Rocking back on his heels, he looked into her gorgeous,

pleasure-sated face. He'd never get tired of seeing her look at him that way.

Her smoky eyes tracked over him. "I knew I could count on you."

He let out a gruff laugh. "I aim to please."

"Good," she hummed, easing out of the office chair with Jeff's help. When she was up, she flashed him another sultry smile. "Up on the desk. You promised."

Hell, yes.

CHAPTER TWENTY-TWO

"YOU DIDN'T ACTUALLY say that," Darcy giggled, her head tipping back as she gave in to the laughter Jeff had a knack for spurring.

The strong hands massaging her right foot stilled. "You *dare* doubt me?"

Sensing her foot rub might be at stake, Darcy offered her best winsome smile and promised, "Never."

At seven-and-a-half months, her feet were feeling the strain of all the baby her body was carrying around, and there wasn't a whole lot she wouldn't do or say to ensure this heavenly attention continued.

Fortunately for her, Jeff had developed the unconscious habit of pulling her feet into his lap every time he dropped onto the couch beside her to talk. And they talked a lot. About whichever project was occupying center stage in her work with his mother, the latest developments at Jeff's company, the psychological thriller they'd watched in bed the night before or their preference of one ethnic cuisine over another and whether they ought to try cooking it or just hit the place around the corner instead.

They talked about the house Jeff had picked out a half mile from his mom's place, and whether Darcy wanted to move in right after the baby was born or whether she wanted to wait a month or so.

And they talked about the baby. Speculating on whether it was a boy or girl and which combination of traits from either of them would be the equivalent of winning the genetics jackpot.

Jeff's take was their kid would be better off with her looks and hair in particular, regardless of whether it was a boy or girl. His singing voice—which was nuts. Her aptitude for quick learning and problem solving. And his brute strength—especially if it was a girl because if she looked like her mother, he wanted her to be able to protect herself like her dad.

Darcy's picks were different. If they got a boy, she wanted him to look like Jeff and a girl she wanted to look like Gail—the fine-boned, feminine version of her son. Beautiful and refined rather than built with too many curves and looks that tended to attract the wrong attention. She wanted their child to have Jeff's sense of humor, drive and generosity. And most of all she wanted this baby to grow up knowing the same kind of love and support that had fostered the happy, confident man across from her.

Jeff grinned, gently rolling her ankle and squeezing her heel. "That's what I thought. Seriously though, Darce, I know it was a work thing, but you should have come with me. Garry's a piece of work, but you would have enjoyed Denise. She's got a six-month-old daughter and a sense of humor like yours and, you know what, they're actually going to be at my table for the benefit next week."

Pushing up against the cushions behind her, Darcy didn't realize she'd begun to pull her foot into her body until Jeff drew it back to his lap.

"Don't pull away," he chided, losing some of the lightness in his expression. "I just thought you might enjoy meeting a few people. Maybe making some friends."

"We've talked about this. I'll make plenty of friends once the baby is born. I just don't want to do it now, as *your date*. I don't want to have to figure out how to explain how we're together and how we aren't, and I know you're not naive enough to think it wouldn't come up. I mean, honestly, Jeff, how would you even introduce me?"

He met her eyes with a hard stare, betraying a frustration that went deeper than this one night. "I'd say 'This is Darcy Penn.'"

"And when they looked at my stomach, or asked how we met, or waited until you were caught up in some discussion about employment trends and then asked me about our relationship?"

"You say we're friends. You say, your house won't be ready to move into for another couple months. You say whatever you're comfortable with."

"That's the thing, Jeff. I'm not comfortable with any of it. Not now. In six months, when your mother is throwing some garden party, and I'm living in my own place and you want us to go together? I'll be fine. You'll be able to introduce me as your son's or daughter's mother. I'll be on my own, actually living the life I'm going to have and not caught in some fairy-tale place I don't want to have to explain the temporary nature of."

He looked like he wanted to argue, but then their in-vitro soccer player took a hard shot at her belly and she flinched, still stunned by the force of those kicks.

Her hand covered the spot and Jeff's attention was immediately fixed on the little world contained within her belly.

"Active?" Abandoning her foot, he shifted closer so he could rest his palms across the hard swell of her stomach.

"I think he liked the roast chicken your mother brought over earlier."

Another kick landed just below Jeff's hand, and Darcy watched his face light with awe and enough tender joy she could feel it in her own chest.

Leaning down, he dropped a kiss against the spot where his hand had been and then turned so his cheek rested lightly there. Darcy stroked his hair, focusing on the bliss of that moment, trying to remember every detail. The warm wash of breath against her skin. The fullness of her belly and her heart.

She wouldn't hope for it to last forever. Only that she remember it when it was gone.

Standing in the doorway of the master bath, Jeff straightened his tie and secured his links. Across the bedroom, Darcy lay half covered with the blanket she couldn't commit to and preferred to keep balled up against her chest, with one leg covered and the other thrown over the top.

She'd finally gotten past the morning sickness, but contrary to how his fantasies had played out, morning was still not her friend. She slept later every day, probably because she was up several times a night thanks to Baby Norton sleeping with one foot on her bladder. And when she woke—

Don't make Hulk angry.

—it was definitely better to give her a few minutes before trying to strike up a conversation.

He'd been seeing her less and less before he left for work. And then thinking about her more and more through those hours they were apart...ultimately leaving the office earlier than his workload required.

Which brought him to his current system. Glancing at the clock, he saw it was four-fourteen. He'd be at his desk by quarter to five and then home a dozen hours later. Which left him as many hours as Darcy had in her in the evenings.

It worked for him.

He was there to see her every day. Be a part of all the doctor visits. The quirky moods and quiet reflections. And around all that—whether she was purring like a kitten or snoring just that side of delicately—she was in his bed. Exactly where he wanted her to be.

Problem was, in just over a month Darcy was going to leave his apartment to have their baby. And when the hospital released her, she wouldn't be coming back. She wanted to move into her own space. No blurry lines regarding the end of their affair.

That's what they'd agreed on.

It had seemed like the easy means of giving Darcy whatever emotional space she needed so she'd still be comfortable sharing physical space with him. So she wouldn't feel trapped or hemmed in. Now that he better understood her past, he was more cognizant than ever of that need to tread carefully.

Only sometime over the past few months, that clear plan with the easy exit strategy had stopped working for him and a new one had begun to take shape. A plan that involved more than blurring the lines.

Leaning down at the edge of the bed, Jeff dropped a light kiss at Darcy's protruding belly and then moved up to do the same at her crown. "Have a good day, gorgeous."

He was going to erase those lines all together. He knew he could. He'd make a success of this unconventional arrangement the way he did with everything else he wanted. Because now that he'd had a taste of what it could be like between them, no way was he going to give that up.

"I thought you said we were going to your mother's?"

Darcy adjusted the pillow at the small of her back watching as Jeff navigated the roads of Bel Air, the look of supreme satisfaction on his face suggesting he was about to burst over *something*.

They were only about a mile from Jeff's mother's house, two from the "little" place Jeff had bought for her and the baby, and headed in the opposite direction. The mystery surrounding their destination making her wonder if he or, more likely, Gail had orchestrated a shower for her despite her protests.

She hoped not, but if that's what it was, she'd be grateful and appreciative because she knew their hearts were in the right place.

"What's this?" she asked when they pulled up to a security gate at a private drive.

Jeff rolled the window down. "Morning, Phil."

The guard offered a quick wave activating the gate, which rolled silently open.

Darcy's eyes landed on the for sale sign posted out front and then looked back at Jeff, nerves kicking up hard in the belly she'd been slowly rubbing.

"Jeff?"

"Wait and see." He flashed her a dazzling grin and her heart started to pound.

A moment later they were parked in front of a breathtaking Spanish Colonial. Jeff hopped out of the car and circled around, that grin going full tilt as he helped her maneuver out of the front seat. Holding her hand, he led her to the open front door.

He didn't knock.

Didn't call a greeting of any sort, just walked a few steps ahead of her, pointing out the soaring ceilings, the wrought iron detail, the oversize formal dining room, the sprawling family room and the top of the line kitchen.

"Did you make an offer on this place?" she asked, afraid to hear the answer. Afraid to find out what they were doing there and why. Afraid to trust the heart that had begun to race dangerously ahead of her mind.

Jeff cocked a brow at her so full of mischief that even in her anxious state, she couldn't help but answer with a laugh.

"Jeff, it's beautiful. Incredible." Enormous. "Are you thinking of making it an investment property?"

"I was thinking it reminded me of all those Spanish-style homes you're always sighing over when we drive around. Only this place was better. Bigger. Eight bedrooms and ten baths…"

He'd been thinking of her.

"…I was thinking it's a house that has everything but the family that belongs in it…"

Oh, God.

Her legs began to shake and she reached for the wall to steady herself, but then Jeff was there, taking her hand and holding it in his.

"...I was thinking we couldn't fill this place yet, but we've got a good start with our little bundle here. And maybe, if you were interested, in another year or so we could think about a brother or sister."

"Jeff," she whispered, her eyes filling with tears, because it couldn't be real and suddenly she knew she wanted it to be with everything she had. It couldn't be—except Jeff was going down on one knee in front of her. Holding her hand in the warm clasp of his, looking at her with eyes filled with expectation, excitement. Happiness.

She'd told herself not to hope for this. Not to let herself believe this was even a possibility, but as she stared down at the man she'd fallen helplessly in love with, she recognized the truth. She'd been a fool to think her heart would end up anywhere but here.

"Darcy, I know this isn't what we talked about. But these past few months, it's been so right having you with me. And as the days get closer to a time when you won't be...I don't even want to think about it. I can't stand the idea of whole days going by when I don't see our child. Of missing every other weekend and every other Christmas morning, when I don't want to miss anything at all. And I know you don't, either."

That thundering heart ground to a halt as Jeff's words hit her. What he was saying. What he wasn't.

He was talking about not wanting to miss out on being a full-time parent. And it was wonderful to know he cared so deeply for their child, but...

Maybe he wasn't done. Maybe as with everything else that happened between them, he was simply using their child as the starting point. Maybe there was more.

Only even as she thought it, disgusting words filled her mind.

You're a fool.

"I know it's not a fairy tale, Darcy, but you said yourself, you weren't interested in one. We get along. We've got chemistry in spades. Sure it's not exactly what either of us imagined our marriage would be, but people make sacrifices for the sake of their children all the time, and I can think of about a million reasons for getting married worse than making a full-time family."

The air felt thin entering her lungs, the edges of her vision starting to haze.

Her throat tightened around all the protests and pleas suddenly desperate to escape. Words she'd never give voice to, because in that moment of sudden grueling clarity, she realized she'd already betrayed herself in all the ways she'd sworn she wouldn't.

"No, it's not the worst reason." The truth was, Darcy hadn't spent a lot of time imagining herself getting married at all. Her fantasies had always been independence-based. But the longer she was with Jeff, the more those fantasies most every other girl had in grade school seemed to flesh out.

The more she started to ache for something they didn't have. "But, Jeff, for me, it's not the right reason, either. I'm sorry, but I can't do this."

CHAPTER TWENTY-THREE

I'M SORRY. THE words hit him like a battering ram to the gut.

The way she'd been looking at him. The way it had been with them the past week. The past months. He'd been sure.

Even now, as he looked into the eyes that had been staring up at him the night before like he was…everything, he couldn't believe it.

He wouldn't.

"Darcy, let's talk about this."

"No, Jeff," she said, pulling her hand from his to hold it trembling against the exaggerated rise and fall of her chest. "Not this time. We agreed."

She was panicking, her eyes darting around like she was searching for escape.

"Okay, slow down, sweetheart. Relax. Yeah, this isn't what we'd agreed on, but I think if we sit a minute and talk it through, you'll see—"

"What will I see? How quickly you can work your magic again?" she asked with a short laugh as the tears he didn't understand began to leak from the corners of her eyes. "How quickly you can figure out some way to tell me just exactly what I need to hear to justify another exception, to get me to bend my rules one more time, to convince me I won't regret it? Here's the problem, Jeff." She jerked back from him, nearly losing her balance and, when he reached to steady her, pushing at his hand. "*I keep believing you.* Through one mistake after another. And now my regrets? I'm trapped behind a wall of them piled so high, I can't even see the life I could have had anymore. The life I *wanted*. And the worst of it is I only have myself to blame...because I knew better!"

They'd driven back to Jeff's apartment in silence. Both absorbing what the other had said. Both wishing, Darcy was certain, they could have taken back their words before they'd been spoken. Taken back the other's, as well.

But if there was one lesson she'd learned, it was there were no take backs.

Once something was done, it couldn't be undone.

All she could do was move forward from there. And her first step, a sorely needed apology.

Jeff was in the living room, his laptop open though he didn't seem to be working on it when she sat opposite him on the couch.

"I shouldn't have said those things to you, Jeff. All you've done from the minute you found out about this baby was try to make things better for me. For us. You've been generous beyond belief. You've been supportive. You've been more than anyone could hope for."

"Don't apologize. You were right. Every time you gave me an inch, I've taken a mile. It wasn't what we agreed to and—hell, I don't know, as the delivery gets closer, I just thought maybe there was a way to make this work."

She shook her head. "It's not you, Jeff."

"No?" He let out a short laugh. "I got the feeling it was."

How could he not. She'd been angry. But more at herself than him. She'd finally seen through all the lies she'd been telling herself about what was happening between them. About how she felt about it and what she could handle. She'd fallen in love. And worse, she'd started to believe Jeff could give her the fairy tale she'd never expected to want.

But the depth of her feelings for him wasn't something she could share. It was information with the power to disrupt their future relationship—one of critical importance. So she would try to tell him the truth, make him understand, without revealing exactly how much he'd taken over her heart.

"You mentioned fairy tales earlier. How I wasn't interested in one anyway. And, for the most part that's been true. As far as destinies went, I wasn't interested in having mine tied to anyone else's. I'd gotten into the habit of looking out for myself. Being on my own. And it worked for me, mostly. But I started seeing things differently after being a part of your family, hearing about what it was like growing up in a home filled with love and respect and caring—the kind of home I'd never known. Not being alone to face every challenge. Having someone there—"

She stopped herself before giving too much away. Shook her head and started again. "I feel like I've been selling myself short my whole life, Jeff. When we met, I'd been on my own for so long, taking care of myself the only way I knew how. Avoiding risks. I'd already started to realize what all my avoidance and caution was costing me. That I was missing out on life, which is why I couldn't resist your offer that first night. I just wanted to live *a little.* But in the months since I've been in L.A.—living with your mom and then with you—I've had a taste of being a part of something bigger. Of something that isn't destructive or about giving things up. Something that makes me feel like *more* instead of less. And it's made me see the possibility of what's out there. What love might be like. You're an incredible man, Jeff. And any woman would be beyond lucky to have you in her life. But we both agree, you and I aren't the fairy tale, and I'm just not ready to resign myself to giving up on finding it yet. I feel like I owe it to myself and to our baby and to you, too, not to let any of us settle for less than we deserve."

And they all deserved so much more than a family founded on sacrifice.

Their child deserved a mother who made a better role model than she'd had herself. Who taught lessons with smiles instead of tears, strength instead of weakness. Bravery instead of fear.

Jeff deserved the kind of marriage his parents had. A wife he saw as a partner, an equal, the other half to make them whole. He deserved to marry someone he loved.

And she deserved more than a lifetime of imbalance in every regard. Loving a man who saw his marriage to her as the sacrifice he'd been willing to make for a "whole" family. She deserved to be able to hope that someday she'd meet someone who made her feel all the things Jeff made her feel, and who would want her for her. Not because a relationship with her would facilitate the full-time parenting package he was really after.

At some point during her explanation, Jeff had moved closer, taking her hand in his own. Now he met her eyes with the kind of understanding that made her wish for all the things she couldn't have with him.

"You're right, Darcy. I promise, no more proposals. Our original agreement stands." Offering a quick grin, he qualified, "Our amended agreement."

She swallowed past this new layer of regret. "I appreciate that. I really do." She tried to shift into a more comfortable position, only this time it wasn't her belly getting in her way. It was her conscience. "But, Jeff, maybe it would be better for both of us, if rather than waiting until the baby comes, I moved out now."

Something dark flashed through his eyes, and she thought he might argue. But instead he simply nodded and with a last gentle squeeze, released her hand. "I'll make some calls and we'll get it done tomorrow."

Darcy stared at the bedroom wall of her new home, telling herself she'd done the right thing.

Jeff had asked her to marry him. Offered to make her his family. To take care of her.

He'd proven time and again, though he didn't love her, he

would treat her like a queen—even going so far as to surprise her with a castle and the crown jewels.

He was beyond generous. Attentive. Caring.

Beautiful in the most rugged way.

Fun and intelligent.

Honest.

Strip away his wealth, and he was still everything she could want in a man. Except for the part about him not feeling quite the same way.

There was no doubt he found her attractive or that he cared for her in a very deep, very real way. But when Jeff had gone looking for a relationship...he'd looked for someone far different from her.

A part of her knew she was crazy to turn him down. But a greater part of her knew she couldn't stand to live like that.

She thought back to all the promises she'd made to herself and knew she'd broken every one...starting the night she'd gone back to Jeff's room. She'd justified and rationalized, for the feel-good of being with a man she'd known from the start wasn't for her. A man who'd warned her he wasn't interested in a relationship, just a few hours of fun. And yeah, later he'd said he'd thought about wanting more. An affair maybe. But for marriage, he'd been looking to Olivia with her social connections, business acumen and impeccable pedigree.

How could she marry a man she knew was settling for her? Making a concession.

She couldn't. She'd done the right thing.

But as the next tear rolled down her cheek, she wondered how she was going to live without him...especially when circumstance assured she'd never be able to get far enough away to forget him.

Jeff stood at his open refrigerator, staring at the second shelf where half a yellow-box-mix cake with fudge frosting sat, abandoned.

He'd bet money Darcy had probably come within a hair's breadth of tears when she realized she'd left it behind. And he'd bet, that had been at about eight-fifteen the evening before.

If he'd been home rather than working through the night at the office, he'd have noticed it there and probably done the same thing he was doing right now. Stood in front of the fridge debating whether he ought to drop it by her place for her.

But somehow the excuse seemed thin, even to him.

Besides if he knew Darcy at all—and despite the failure of his proposal and her subsequent exodus from his apartment as a result, he did—she'd already have taken care of whatever box mix needs she'd had on her own.

Just the way she liked it.

Pulling the phone from his pocket, he checked to see if she'd texted. Even set to near Richter-five vibration with a ringtone to match, it was possible he'd missed her call or text.

Only he hadn't.

He opened the fridge again. Laughed a little when he noticed the suspicious marks from fork tines in the frosting— but then the sound of his laughing alone in a space that had been filled with Darcy just two days before made his chest ache and all the humor evaporated into the still silent air around him.

He could *just call* and see if she wanted him to bring the cake. Maybe she hadn't thought to put a box mix on the list for the housekeeper he'd hired to shop and do all the things eight-months-pregnant women weren't comfortable doing. Sure there was a driver on call for her 24/7. And if she'd been up for going to his mother's today, she might have found a box there…but what if she hadn't.

What if she was hungry?

What if the only reason she wasn't calling to ask about the cake was because she felt like she shouldn't after moving out? What if she thought *he* didn't want to hear from *her?*

Okay, and what if he never got a grip again.

If Darcy wanted to talk to him, she'd call. If she wanted cake, she'd make one.

If she wanted him...hell. She'd still be here. In his arms. In his bed. In his life in a way that wasn't simply about waiting for their child to be born so they could share it like civilized adults.

And she wasn't.

CHAPTER TWENTY-FOUR

"Darcy, don't you make me take that file from you. It's nearly seven."

Hand flat on the top of the file in question, Darcy shook her head. "You even think about taking this from me, and you can kiss your 'Nana Gail' fantasies goodbye. I'll have this baby calling you Gammy Gigi for years."

Jeff's mother flinched, but apparently tonight she wasn't backing down. Slipping her phone from her pocket, she made a show of starting to text. "Hold on, dear. Let's talk about this in a moment. After I tell Jeff about how you aren't eating and you look so very pale."

"What?" she gasped, grabbing the plate with the remains of her organic burrito...the second burrito, because there wasn't even a single crumb left to show for the first. "This is my third, no, fourth meal today. Since I've been here!"

Gail didn't look up as she sighed. "We old people get so easily confused. The file, Darcy."

Old. At fifty-five, Gail was hardly material for the old folks' home, especially since she had the physique and attitude of a woman closer to forty. Add another item to her ever-growing "Why I want to be like Gail when I grow up" list.

Darcy looked down. She knew it had been a long day, but the truth was, being at home was difficult. It was beautiful and comfortable and all, but a week into living there, she still found herself watching the clock for the part of her day that had become her favorite, waiting for an event that wasn't going to come.

Reminding herself that Jeff wouldn't be swinging through the door at any moment.

It was just her. Alone. With nothing to wait for or anticipate at the day's end because she'd had to go and make the smart decision for herself. And it stunk.

She used to thrive on living by herself. But that was before she'd had a taste of what it felt like to share a home. Before Jeff.

"I wonder what he'll do when he hears how sad and thin and worn-out you look?"

Darcy narrowed her eyes. She did not look thin. The rest, possibly. But certainly not enough to report to Jeff. Gail was bluffing.

And if she wasn't...

No, she tamped down that insidious little hopeful part of her looking for any excuse or justification to see him. Anything to ease this hollow aching part of her that had opened up the day she moved out and secured his promise to give her some space as they adjusted to the new phase of their relationship. They'd be seeing each other soon enough once the baby arrived.

But Gail *was* bluffing because no matter what Darcy and Jeff had respectively told her about Darcy's move to her new place, Gail wasn't stupid. She wasn't blind. And she wasn't one to manipulate her son for sport. So no worries. That text wasn't going anywhere.

Still this was the most entertainment she'd had since ripping her heart in half when she moved out of Jeff's place. Maybe she wasn't ready to give it up just yet.

"You do that, and I'll tell him...I'll tell him..." What lie she'd never actually tell could she threaten Gail with—ha! She had it. "I'll tell him Grant put a move on *you!* You'll have that promising young doctor's blood all over your hands. So how about them apples, Gail?"

Darcy waited for the gasp, the cough, the laugh or the escalated threat, anticipating whatever the response with glee.

Ready for whatever her friend had to lob back at her. But all she got was Gail staring at her, wide-eyed and stock-still.

The seconds stretched, and Darcy's brows began to creep skyward. "No. Way."

Gail blinked, looked down at the floor where she made a small circle with the toe of her shoe. Finally she shrugged. "Give me the file and I'll tell you about it."

Three things ran through her mind at once.

First, Grant didn't value his life the way she would have expected him to.

Second, Wow. No wonder Jeff didn't know how to lose.

And third, rename her list as "Why Gail is my hero" and add this as the top line item.

Handing over the file, she tried not to think about what ran through her mind next. How relieved she was not to have to be heading back to her lonely house. How grateful she was for what would probably be the only distraction powerful enough to keep her mind off the man she couldn't stop missing.

The door swung open and Connor squinted out at him. "Not that I'm not happy to see you. But it's four in the morning, Jeff. What are you doing here?"

Yeah, what indeed. Trying to keep himself from making a seriously monumental mistake. And calling in a favor to do it.

"Needed to get out of the apartment for a while. So I went for a drive. Ended up in the neighborhood. Thought I'd stop in."

"Two hundred miles is a bit of a drive."

"Yeah."

"You look like hell."

Jeff gave Connor a once-over, taking in the bedhead that put the other man's hair on par with his own, the wrinkle running across his cheek and the unfocused look in general. "Coming from you, that's saying something."

"Ha. So you want to come in, or was this just a drive-by?"

"I need you to take my phone. Darcy asked me to give her some space. And I'm trying. Really, really hard. But I haven't seen her in two weeks. And even though I've talked to my mom and Grant and they both say she's doing great, I haven't seen her. Not being able to—hell, the only reason I'm not knocking on her door right now is because I forced myself to turn left instead of right…and keep going. And the only way I'm not going to call her and tell her that I can't stand another damn day like this…when I need to be able to stand a whole damn lifetime like it, is if you take the damn phone out of my damned hand. *Please.*"

Connor looked down at the offending piece of technology and held out his hand for it.

"Thank you," he said as Connor waved him inside.

"I owed you one, right?"

Jeff was about to make the usual polite protest—even though it was the absolute truth—when he stopped at the sound of crunching plastic and metal.

Eyes bugging, he cranked his head around to where Connor was pulling the crushed phone from between the door and the frame, a sleepy half-cocked grin on his face as he handed back what had seconds before been a working phone, painstakingly programmed to accommodate every aspect of his life. At his stunned stare, Connor slapped the bits of phone into his palm and said, "Now we're even. And you're welcome."

Five minutes later, Connor set five bottles between them, then dropped into the kitchen chair, eyeing Jeff over the table. "Let's get this out of the way first. What kind of night are we having? Coffee?" he asked, holding a hand over the two bottles of caramel-and-cream flavored iced coffee, before moving to hover over the green glass of his favorite imports. "Beer?"

Then rubbing a hand over his mouth and the scrub of his jaw, Connor eyed the last bottle warily. "Or if it's really, really bad…and only for you…" He winced, looking away. "This."

A twenty-five-year-old Scotch Jeff was willing to bet Connor hadn't had a glass of since the night Jeff had had to run out of a meeting to head him off at the airport before Connor showed up drunk at his then-estranged wife's door.

"Wow. You really do love me," Jeff said, and grabbed the hard stuff as he pushed back from the table and set the bottle at the far counter. Looking back at Connor, he turned the bottle so the label wasn't staring him down like some school yard bully. "But I love you, too, and even if I didn't— do you honestly think I'm going to get plowed with my pregnant non-girlfriend God only knows where? Doing God only knows what. With God only knows who."

"Isn't she with your mom?"

"No. She's at her new house. Probably sleeping. Alone." Of course alone. Definitely alone. For now.

And as soon as that thought hit him, the next certainty followed.… If she didn't want to be alone, she wouldn't have to be. He saw the way guys looked at her, eight months pregnant or not. Hell, he knew how he looked at her. How he wanted her.

How he missed her.

"I'll pass on the beer, too," he said, but scowled at the remaining selection of iced coffee. "Caramel?"

"Megan bought it. The machine is broken, just man up and drink what's on offer. It's actually pretty good."

Reluctantly, Jeff grabbed his own and tried it. Smacked his lips. "Like liquid candy."

Connor gave him an I-told-you-so look and settled back in his chair with a bottle of the iced coffee. "Okay. So now that we've got the beverage portion of the evening—err, morning—out of the way. Let's have it. What's going on?"

"I asked Darcy to marry me." At Connor's raised brows, he added, "She declined."

"Aw hell, I'm sorry, Jeff. I didn't realize it was like that with you two. Or at least that you'd realized it was—and I'm probably not helping, either. Okay, why'd she say no?"

Jeff ran a finger through the condensation on his bottle, wondering how it was possible to feel half numb and wholly horrible all at once. "The first time, because she didn't *care* about 'the whole legitimacy thing.'"

"Umm, out of curiosity, how many times did she turn you down?"

He shoved his hands through his hair. "A couple. Few maybe. Once because I asked like I was joking around. I know. Big surprise. And okay, then because I asked when she was throwing up."

"Dude," Connor gasped, pulling away in his chair even as he said it.

"Yeah, yeah." Jeff waved at the air. He'd been trying to cheer her up but, yeah. He knew. "And most recently, because she thinks she can do better."

The coffee clanked on the table as Connor threw up his hands, all what's-this-world-coming-to? "She thinks she can do better than *you?* What the hell is she looking for? You're generous, kind, almost as intelligent as I am, not quite as good-looking, but what you lack in pretty you make up in portfolio."

Jeff let out a short laugh, but the real thing seemed harder and harder to come by these days. "Connor, no matter how you sweet-talk me, I'm not getting in bed with you again. So don't even try."

"Someone's still smarting over me thinking he was Megan," Connor responded in a deep singsong voice that really should have made Jeff's day. "And nice dodge, but aside from the nose and hair, you're like every woman's idea of Mr. Right. I'm serious, man. What does she want?"

Jeff took his own drink, only the sugary concoction had turned sour on his tongue. "She wants to be in love with the guy she marries."

Connor rocked back in his seat. And who could blame

him. There wasn't much room for outrage with a defense like that.

"She said she doesn't love you?"

Jeff pinched the bridge of his nose, thinking about all the times Darcy had pushed him away. Walked out on him. Told him she didn't want what he was offering. He thought of that last conversation, the way she'd looked at him with such regret in her eyes as she told him she couldn't marry him because… "She didn't have to."

He cleared his throat and met Connor's concerned stare. "Which was fine. It wasn't like that with us."

Connor's brows pinched together, concern turning to calculation in a blink, as he drawled, "Oh, really?"

Jeff shifted uncomfortably. Whatever that look was, he didn't like being on the receiving end of it. "Knock it off, Connor."

"I don't know what you're talking about."

"I got her pregnant. I didn't fall in love with her. It was never about love. It was about making a family. I'm upset because it didn't work out like I'd hoped."

More of that look. "Sure."

"Damn it, Connor. This isn't like you and Megan."

"Didn't say it was."

"You're looking at me…with this infuriatingly…*smug* look. And it's making me want to mess up your perfect nose."

Totally unconcerned, Connor reached across the table, his crooked smile smug and secure as he rubbed his hand over the top of Jeff's head.

Condescension and delight mixing in his voice, he said, "I love you, man. But come on, I can't believe you don't see what I've been hearing in your voice for months. In every mention of her. Every frustration, every funny story, every TMI account you can't seem to contain. And if you can't hear it in your own words, then maybe it's time you take a good look at why exactly you are so hell-bent on getting this woman to marry you. You keep asking her for everything, but I'm not sure you're seeing all you've got to give in return. Which means maybe she's not seeing it, either."

No. Connor was just reading his own happy ending into Jeff's story. But it wasn't that way. They'd agreed up front about the limits so no one would get the wrong idea. It had worked with every other relationship he'd had since Margo. And granted none of those women had held a candle to Darcy. They'd been easy to say goodbye to in a way he couldn't even contemplate with Darcy...but still.

Jeff collapsed back in his chair, the weight on his chest one of unwilling recognition. "Hell."

Connor was right. But unfortunately, that didn't change a damn thing as far as Darcy wanting to marry him. Or live with him. Or see him. Or talk to him. Or laugh with him. Or any of the million other things Jeff wanted to do with her.

That was the heart of it. He wanted everything.

While she wanted to be friendly, independent co-parents to the child they would share for the rest of their lives...he wanted the fairy tale.

And he'd promised Darcy he wouldn't ask for it.

CHAPTER TWENTY-FIVE

THERE WAS SOMETHING distinctly unsatisfying about going for a drive to clear your head when you were stuck in the backseat behind a paid driver. Who wouldn't give up the wheel, even for a pregnant woman threatening tears.

Why the hell had she turned down Jeff's offer to buy her a car.

Her throat tightened as she wondered, not for the first time and with disturbingly increasing frequency, why she'd turned him down for anything. She loved him. And he'd offered to marry her. But because she couldn't have everything *just exactly the way she wanted it,* because she was too spoiled, too greedy, too selfish...she'd said no.

And then to top it off, because it felt *too good* being in his arms, his bed and his home...she'd moved out.

Every day her body grew, filling her more with the child they'd made together. And every day she went without Jeff, she felt like a bigger piece of her was missing.

All the regrets she'd thrown in his face that horrible last day together...there was only one she could see now. And there was no one to blame for it but herself.

She let out a heavy sigh and then spoke to the driver. "Harvey, I know I said we weren't going today, but could you take me to Gail's, please."

For as much as she'd avoided discussing her relationship with Jeff out of respect for all of them, she needed some advice. Because staying away from him felt more wrong by the minute. And not just because of how much it hurt not to be with him, but because he'd wanted to be a part of her pregnancy and share in the experience. And asking him to stay away, to give her space so she could try to get over him wasn't fair. And more than that, it wasn't going to work.

The drive up from San Diego at rush hour had taken twice the time it took to drive down in the middle of the night, but time to think wasn't necessarily the worst thing and Jeff accepted whatever traffic holdups the highway gods had in store for him without question. That is until he'd gotten to his mother's neighborhood and watched an ambulance fly by him, lights flashing, siren going full blast.

Instinctively he reached for his phone, but only came back with a handful of broken technology and a choice expletive with Connor's name on it.

As soon as the emergency vehicle passed, he hit the gas, telling himself it was going to turn off before his mom's place. Either that or roll right past. Sure Darcy was getting close, but those lights weren't for her. It wasn't the baby. It wasn't the end of his world. It couldn't be.

Please, no.

Only as his mother's drive came into view and the ambulance was already disappearing down it, that kernel of dread in his gut became a cannonball and the fantasy it was just his world that would end if something happened to Darcy went up in smoke. It would be the end of his universe. A loss so great, the limits were beyond comprehension.

Hands gripping the wheel tight enough that they threatened to rip it off, Jeff focused on that final stretch of road. Pulling up the drive. Slamming the car into Park as his mother, looking wild and desperate, pulled one of the responders with her around the far side of the house.

And then Jeff was out of the car, running across the lawn, trying to make a throat seized with panic work so he could call out, demand to know what happened.

The small group was huddled together between the house and a flower bed. The EMTs kneeling beside—

"Really, I don't need an ambulance. It's just a sprain. *I'm a doctor.*"

Skidding to a stop, the air punched out of his lungs as Grant's voice sounded above the rest.

What the hell?

Only then whatever was happening with Grant became secondary, as one fact washed over him with tsunami force.

Not Darcy.

He saw her, struggling up from her knees where she'd been on the ground next to Grant. One hand supporting her belly as she found her balance and looked up, meeting his eyes as he took those last desperate steps and caught her against him.

"Darcy." Her name was gravel-rough when he managed to get it past his throat. "You're okay."

"Jeff, look at your face." And he could see from the look on hers, that his must be reflecting exactly the soul-deep horror he'd been experiencing. "The baby's fine. I swear, we're okay."

He nodded, trying not to hold her too tightly, but having her in his arms after weeks without, finding her safe after seeing that ambulance—it was all he could do not to crush her against him and make her swear she'd never leave his arms again. Only that wasn't what he'd come for, and based on the scene around him, circumstances might not allow for him to make any kind of claim at all.

His eye shifted to Grant who, despite the fact there was an ambulance there for him, seemed to be doing okay.

But what was he doing there at ten in the morning midweek? He hadn't needed to check on Darcy since she'd started seeing her regular doctor months ago. But then maybe the reason Grant was here wasn't professional. Maybe he'd found out Darcy had moved into her own place and decided to make his move before any of the other vultures swooped in.

Smart. But it made Jeff wish the guy looked a little worse off than he actually seemed to be.

"What happened?" he asked as Darcy buried her head against his chest.

"It's my fault," she started. "I'd told your mother I didn't think I'd be in this morning, but then I came over anyway. And when I closed the door——"

"Calm down, Gail," Grant urged, his voice overriding Darcy's whisper. "I know you're worried, but I'm telling you, it's a sprained knee and——"

"Don't you, 'Calm down, Gail,' me. You're the damned fool who decided to climb out the window and fell. A second-story window, Grant. I already lost one man I loved and I'm not about to let your dinged-up pride cause me to lose you, too."

Jeff choked on the breath he'd been taking, sure beyond any reason he hadn't just heard that right.

"Mom?"

His mother's head snapped around suggesting she'd only just realized he was there. For an instant her eyes registered the kind of shock and nerves one would expect—but then this was his mother. And in the next instant, those eyes flashed steel. "Not now, honey."

Jeff felt the span of Darcy's hands pressing into his chest, as though she meant to hold him back, which was adorable in itself. But unnecessary. He wasn't going anywhere.

"Grant and my mom?" he asked. All those times the guy mentioned how limber she seemed… He'd assumed Grant's mind was on osteoporosis. But apparently not.

"I guess he's had a thing for her…forever. The night he was going to take us out, really had been about spending more time with Gail. And I guess it worked." Darcy looked uneasy. "This morning Connor called asking if you'd arrived. When they heard the door downstairs a minute later, assuming it was you rather than me, Grant decided the window seemed like his best chance for survival."

Jeff took a deep breath, savoring the feminine scent of Darcy's shampoo and lotion and the woman beneath.

"Okay."

"Okay?" she asked, sounding skeptical.

"Darcy, I'm not going to attack the guy on his way into the ambulance." When she looked at him seemingly unconvinced, he added, "My mother would kill me."

And after all the weeks, he got what he'd missed the most. A flash of the gorgeous smile that started it all. The one he'd never get over. The one he still wanted to earn.

Grant grudgingly agreed to let the ambulance take him to the hospital to get checked out and Gail went along with him, leaving Jeff and Darcy at the house alone.

Since getting her into his arms, Jeff hadn't been able to let go. And Darcy seemed to understand, settling against him.

Damn, it felt so good to be standing beside her. To have his hands on her.

But as the ambulance disappeared down the drive, Darcy took the hand anchoring his arm across her chest and, with a light squeeze, extracted herself from his hold.

"Want to go inside?" she asked, looking more nervous now that the emergency had passed and it was back to just the two of them.

Jeff gave her a stiff nod, then looked back to his car, half parked on the grass, the door gaping wide from when he'd bolted out for the house.

"Let me pull around back. And I'll meet you there."

Darcy started to go, then paused and turned back, asking, "Are you okay?"

Not even a little bit. Not yet. "Give me a few minutes and I will be."

By the time Darcy made it back to the kitchen, Jeff had parked and was bringing in a breathtaking vase of flowers and a white pastry box, both of which looked as though they'd taken a hit during their stint in Jeff's car.

Still, Gail would be touched by the thoughtful gesture when she got back from the hospital.

Jeff, looking as weary and worn and sexy and compelling as he had that night after his return from Australia, set his load on the counter, and kept walking toward her.

"I know you wanted space and I know I just let you go, but, Darcy— I need— I thought— I'm so glad—"

She went to him, understanding the kind of fear he must have been feeling. Wanting to offer him whatever comfort she could.

Reaching for his hands she pulled them to the round swell of her belly, pressing them flat. "He's fine," she promised. And when a swift little kick met the warm spot covered by Jeff's open palm, she laughed—all the relief that Jeff was here, all the love and all the nerves bubbling up inside her at once. Finding release in that short moment.

Jeff stared down at the spot he was now rubbing in a soft circle. He gave her belly one last pat.

"Darcy, I'm relieved our baby is safe. Of course I am… but—" his voice broke, and shaking his head he cupped her jaw, and then met her eyes with a tortured look "—when I thought something might have happened to *you,* my God, I couldn't breathe. I couldn't think."

The way he was looking at her—what he was saying. It wasn't the way it sounded. She was seeing what she wanted to see, hearing what she wanted to hear, reading meaning that didn't exist again.

This time she knew better.

She offered the back of his hand a gentle stroke, wanting to remember the feel of it forever, and then stepped back.

Instead of letting her heart run away from her, she held firm to the reality she knew to be true.

Jeff cared about her. Of that there had never been a doubt.

And if ever there was a moment she had the chance to secure the same offer he'd made to her three weeks before—to make her his wife, make them a family—this was it. He'd been afraid of losing them and knowing Jeff, right now the man would probably do anything—say anything—promise anything to make that feeling go away.

Which was why right now wasn't the time to talk to him about the possibility of them being together in some capacity. Of finding out what kind of arrangement would give them all what they wanted. Or as close to it as was possible.

She'd done it again. Pulled away from him. Given him another obvious cue she didn't want what he was offering.

The right thing to do would be to leave her be. But damn it, doing the "right thing" with Darcy always felt so wrong.

He'd been curbing his impulses from the word *go*. Trying to find compromise by taking more than he should without going after all that he wanted. By lying to both of them about what would be enough.

Letting Darcy down every step of the way.

He'd thought he'd been honest with her.

Thought he'd been fair. But the truth was, with every concession he'd made, some secret dark part of him had known he'd be going back for more.

That time was over.

"How have you been?" It seemed trite, but Jeff hadn't seen her in weeks. They hadn't been talking. And he wanted to know.

Darcy went to the sink and started filling a kettle. "We've been doing pretty well. Getting used to the new house. Settled in. How about you?"

Jeff pulled out a kitchen chair and sat down at it, watching as Darcy made tea. "I've been lonely. Missing you. Wishing I'd done about a thousand things differently and wondering if any of them would have gotten me an outcome other than this."

The kettle clattered against the stove top and Darcy grabbed the counter behind her.

Every part of Jeff wanted to go to her, usher her into a seat or, better, his lap. But he'd been taking what he wanted with Darcy from the start, pushing for his end goal without giving her the chance to decide what she wanted. He had to stop, for both of them. He wanted Darcy confident in the choices she made so they didn't end up feeling like regrets trapping her in a place she didn't want to be. So despite every instinct trying to drag him across the kitchen to go to her, hold her, use his body along with his words to get what he wanted…he made himself stay.

There was only one thing he could give her right now, and that was the truth.

"I've been working eighteen-hour days trying to keep myself distracted enough so I won't start formulating my next plan to get you back, plotting what I can say to convince you to bend your rules just a little to suit my needs. I'm exhausted. I'm miserable. And I'm thinking if I want any chance at the happiness I know we can have together, I need to start figuring out how to be the man you deserve. The one you can trust and count on. Who makes you laugh. Makes you feel safe. And most of all, makes you want to stay instead of leave."

"Jeff, when we talked last time—" She looked at him like she was terrified, her hands gripping the countertops at either side of her like they were the only things holding her upright. "Maybe today isn't the day to talk about this."

He wanted to be what she leaned on. The support she never doubted. Always.

"Don't worry. I'm not asking you to marry me again."

She nodded tightly, looking miserable and confused. And it was so damned hard not to go to her that very second.

"I promised you I wouldn't, and I'm going to be a man you can count on to keep his word." He cleared his throat then and met her eyes. "But I *am* going to ask you what I came here to ask today. If you'd give me a chance to take you out on a date."

Darcy blinked, not sure she'd heard right. "A date?" Her heart started to speed because he'd said a *date* and there weren't a lot of ways to misinterpret that word. And still she was using every bit of her rapidly diminishing self-control to hold herself in check, not to sail into his arms if he meant something else.

He was talking about missing her. About wishing things were different. But the way he'd said it didn't sound so very different from when he'd asked her to marry him the last time when it was all about wanting to be together for the sake of their child.

At least it hadn't sounded different until he'd gotten to the part where he asked for a date.

Which was...different. "A date, date? Or *just* a date...or maybe a date that doesn't mean what I think it means but—"

"A date, like I want to make you fall in love with me, date," Jeff answered, his voice steady even as he stared at his hands. "And okay, so that's maybe a lot of pressure up front, but I'm through telling you all I want is one thing, when the truth is I want everything. I want you to marry me, but I get—"

"Why? So you can be with our child each night?" The words burst past her lips, not in accusation but because she just needed to know. "It's okay if that's why...."

He met her eyes and what she saw in his stole her breath, made her grip the counter tighter still. Not to hold herself back—but to hold herself up. Because what she saw when he looked at her like that was enough to floor her completely.

"Because *I love you.*"

Her lips parted, but whatever words she'd thought to say or breath she'd meant to take didn't come. All she could do was stare, wait for whatever he had to say next. Because she couldn't believe him yet. She was terrified and yet some part of her must have made the decision to do just that, because suddenly she wasn't holding on to the counter anymore. She was crossing the kitchen to the man who was staring at her like he'd just witnessed a miracle.

And then she was standing in the V of his legs, her hands were in the gorgeous unruly mess of his hair, her breath coming in broken little gasps.

"You love me?"

He swallowed and offered her a nod. "I think I have from the very first night, Darcy, I just couldn't let myself admit it. When I realized you were gone in Vegas—it rocked me. But I tried to tell myself it was no big deal. It couldn't be. We'd just met. I'd forget about you. Only instead of forgetting, I kept thinking about you. Wondering how I could have misjudged what was going on between us so badly."

"I'm so sorry," she started, wishing again she could go back, wondering how differently things would have gone if she'd stayed. If they'd kept in touch. "I was afraid of what you made me feel after we'd agreed to what kind of night it would be."

"I know, sweetheart. But at the time, and even after we were together again, I kept thinking this is a woman who leaves. A woman who keeps putting her hand up and telling me not to get any closer. And even though it didn't keep me from pushing past those boundaries we kept agreeing to... it was enough for me to use as an excuse to keep from owning up to the truth. That first night with you changed something in me, made me want more than I'd been settling for in my relationships."

"And you found Olivia."

"She seemed like such a smart fit...except for the part where she wasn't you."

Darcy buried her head against Jeff's shoulder, holding on to him so tight. "Everything I heard about her, she was different from me. And everyone said you two were serious.

Perfect for each other. That it was just a matter of time. And all I could think was she was everything I wasn't. I couldn't see myself as anything but a sacrifice so you could make your family work."

"*No.* I shouldn't have said it. I shouldn't have tried to make either of us believe it."

She wrapped her arms around his neck and stared into his eyes.

"So you really love me?"

"I really do."

"That's good. Because I've been falling for you from the start, and no matter how I've tried to stop it…nothing could. I love you, too."

Jeff kissed her then. Slow and tender and sweet and perfect. When they broke away, half breathless with desire, Darcy asked, "So what do we do now?"

Jeff nodded toward the counter. "I give you those flowers I brought for you, and woo you into letting me take you out by bribing you with that yellow-box-mix cake I made for you at Connor's, and then I romance you until you beg me to marry you."

Darcy laughed, her brows high. "I'm supposed to ask you?"

Very seriously, Jeff kissed her again. Then answered, "I'm a man you can count on. I promised you I wouldn't ask again. But—" He leaned closer and whispered in her ear, "I'm a sure thing. So whenever you feel safe. Whenever you feel solid about it. Tell me and—"

"Marry me, Jeff."

He blinked at her, the corner of his mouth kicking up into a sexy grin that was all mayhem and mischief. "Why?"

She gasped. "You just told me you'd say yes!"

"Oh, you better believe I'm going to say yes. But you asked why. So I'm asking."

Laying her hand over his heart and taking his to rest over their growing baby, she nodded. "Because I love you.

And you make me believe in happily ever afters. So say yes, please."

"Yes."

Two weeks later.

Her body heavy with fatigue, Darcy opened her eyes in the dim light of her hospital room to the most precious sight of her life. Her husband, leaning over eight-pound-one-ounce Garrison Jeffrey Norton as he affixed the tiny diaper in place, straightened the little hospital shirt and then, cradling him close, moved into the chair by the bed.

Arranging their son so Darcy could see him clearly, he took off the tiny knit cap revealing a dark brown shock of hair so wild, it made even his daddy's look tame. "Just look at what we made, Darcy. Can you believe it?"

"Our family," she murmured, her heart overflowing with love for this precious gift they'd been granted. For the man looking between her and their child with such unabashed adoration, such love, it took her breath away. Reaching out to stroke that silky fuzz, she smiled. "Our beautiful Happily Ever After."

Jeff looked down at his boy with pride and then shot her his most devastating grin, made even more so by the utter fatigue showing over every inch of him. "Our first one. What do you say we see about trying for a girl with your hair next."

* * * * *

Mills & Boon® Hardback
March 2014

ROMANCE

A Prize Beyond Jewels	Carole Mortimer
A Queen for the Taking?	Kate Hewitt
Pretender to the Throne	Maisey Yates
An Exception to His Rule	Lindsay Armstrong
The Sheikh's Last Seduction	Jennie Lucas
Enthralled by Moretti	Cathy Williams
The Woman Sent to Tame Him	Victoria Parker
What a Sicilian Husband Wants	Michelle Smart
Waking Up Pregnant	Mira Lyn Kelly
Holiday with a Stranger	Christy McKellen
The Returning Hero	Soraya Lane
Road Trip With the Eligible Bachelor	Michelle Douglas
Safe in the Tycoon's Arms	Jennifer Faye
Awakened By His Touch	Nikki Logan
The Plus-One Agreement	Charlotte Phillips
For His Eyes Only	Liz Fielding
Uncovering Her Secrets	Amalie Berlin
Unlocking the Doctor's Heart	Susanne Hampton

MEDICAL

Waves of Temptation	Marion Lennox
Risk of a Lifetime	Caroline Anderson
To Play with Fire	Tina Beckett
The Dangers of Dating Dr Carvalho	Tina Beckett